Dead Editor File

By

G G Collins

Chamisa Canyon Publishing
chamisacanyon@live.com
Attn: Rights & Permissions

Book Cover & Interior by Vila Design
Editing by Jay Terre

ISBN-13 978-0-9884674-6-0
ISBN-13 978-0-9884674-8-4 (ebook)

Books by G G Collins

Reluctant Medium
Lemurian Medium
Atomic Medium
Presence: A Rachel Blackstone Paranormal Mystery Short Story
Dead Editor File
Looking Glass Editor
Murder USA: A Crime Fiction Tour of the Nation (anthology, contributor)
Flying Change
Without Notice

Forthcoming

Anasazi Medium
Editorial Kill Fee

AUTHOR'S NOTE

Publishing is a complex industry, at once creative and yet a business. The myriad of details that must be accomplished before a book can be published is difficult to comprehend, especially to the author waiting in the wings.

On average, an author will spend several months to a year writing a book. Whether traditionally or indie published, there are many decisions along the way: white or cream paper, gloss or matte cover, font choice and cover art. Marketing includes sales rep presentation, ARC (advance review copy; also referred to as a galley), choosing reviewers and requesting interviews. Steps to publication include editing, typesetting, blueline, proofs and finally a book you can hold in your hands. It can take a year to publication unless the publisher fast tracks it because it's topical or urgent reading.

Daily life at a book publisher can range from deadly quiet to abject chaos, all the while processing the hundreds to thousands of manuscripts and queries that arrive daily. More queries are submitted via email, but some writers still use the mail route. Envelopes and boxes holding the blood, sweat and tears of writers are stacked on desks, office floors, hallways and in closets. Most are returned unread by unpaid interns with a form letter and are never seen by editors.

Writers write because they must; because they have stories to tell. Make an author's day and write a short review describing why you liked—or loved their book. The next time you pick up a book, know it was a very long journey to your hands.

ACKNOWLEDGEMENTS & GRATITUDE

My thanks to Terry who has acted as my first reader for years and continues to brainstorm with me over dinner and drinks while I'm writing down ideas as fast as I can hoping my dinner doesn't get cold.

Much appreciation to my friends who support and encourage me: Cheryl, Judi and Marilyn.

To Santa Fe, New Mexico, a city rich in history and three cultures, for providing a beautiful and intriguing background.

Del Charro Saloon is a real restaurant in Santa Fe, found in the Inn of the Governors. It is popular with both visitors and locals. Located on the corner of West Alameda and Don Gaspar, you can watch the world go by or catch the score while enjoying food and margaritas. Pssst. Their green chile is wonderful!

For Judi
Wonderful friend; intrepid traveler.

"Much publishing is done through politics, friends and natural stupidity."

— Charles Bukowski, American Author

Chapter 1

"**C**an't you do anything right?" yelled Preston Endicott, Jr. at his newest secretary. He looked heavenward and spread his arms wide to emphasize his dramatic tantrum. "Is it not possible to find competent help these days?" he said in his best booming theatrical voice.

Alise's bright blue eyes brimmed with tears. The employment counselor told her he was a difficult boss, but she'd never expected to be subjected to such wrath on the second day of her new job. She was competent. *She was!* Her administrative assistant skills were above average and she prided herself with getting along with everyone.

Endicott's face had taken on an angry blush and his veins bulged dangerously. Alise's legs threatened to fold if he reached another decibel. Instead they carried her quickly away from the tirade, down the long hallway, where every door had been discreetly closed, to the stairs.

It was four o'clock. She still had an hour to call the employment office before it closed. Maybe they could find her another job; one where yelling would be kept to a minimum.

"Hey, I want this mess cleaned up!" Endicott swept a handful of mail from his desk onto the hardwood floor. "Do you hear me?" he bellowed. Alise would have to be in another county not to.

There was no answer from the fleeing young woman, only the sound of her footsteps down the stairs.

"I have to do everything myself," he muttered picking up the scattered mail. It was impossible to slam the heavy, carved door to his office, but he was able to get a thud if not an actual slam.

Endicott stomped across the beautiful Oriental rug. He bought it only because the carpet was expensive and auspicious, not because he liked it. His office had the air of power. A sprawling mahogany paneled desk was topped with a sheet of glass. There were no mementos under the glass. He was not sentimental.

"I can't stand anymore incompetence today," he told the downstairs receptionist over the intercom. "I am not to be disturbed!"

"Yes Mr. Endicott," she replied. Candi had worked at Endicott Publishing for four years and knew better than to say anything else, especially after witnessing a tearful Alise run through the lobby.

Endicott tossed his mail, expertly opened by the woman he'd just sent scuttling away, onto the blotter and stood looking out the balcony doors. When he sat down heavily in the dark leather chair it creaked in response to his weight. He was not an overweight man but tall, at least 6 feet, 6 inches. He had an imposing presence—usually provoking wariness, if not fear.

The first envelope obviously contained his electric bill, and the second he knew was from his ex-wife, Jessica, a reminder of his late alimony payment. Although it was old-school, since most book queries now arrive via email, she always included a self-addressed, stamped envelope for him to use when he sent her check. He presumed she thought it a joke. He took his checkbook from the center drawer, wrote checks, jammed them into envelopes and sealed each one himself with a flourish.

"Ah, more hopefuls." Using his thumb he tore open several large, manila envelopes containing queries from optimistic writers still using this method of submission. They were addressed to him personally. Normally they went through editorial. But these writers had taken the time to look up the big cheese. Each held samples of a writer's work, submitted after exhausting hours writing and rewriting both the manuscript and the accompanying cover letter. Most of the time they were returned. When everything worked in synergy the writer would get an acceptance letter with contract to follow. Not these authors.

Endicott himself was published—mostly business articles—but he didn't give a hoot about these writers. He was in no mood to be pleased by anything he read. "These things should have gone to an editor anyway." He sniffed.

Usually he let his assistant or the appropriate editor screen queries, but he felt particularly punitive at the moment and since the object of that feeling had jumped ship he would take it out on some unsuspecting wannabes. Endicott pronounced each query "Garbage, junk and trash." He unceremoniously crammed the material into the return envelopes, threw in a prepared rejection slip, licked each envelope seal and dropped them on his desk. Everything else was tossed into the trash.

Endicott leaned back in his chair, arms crossed over his chest. "I'll fire that hussy tomorrow if she dares to show her face at all."

He made one more trip to Alise's desk, dropped his payments in the outgoing mail, returned to his office. With a quick poke of his thumb, he locked the door. He was in no hurry to mail the queries. They could sit on his desk for awhile.

* * *

The following morning, Taylor Browning was late but didn't realize it yet. She was trying on her new outfit—the so-called southwest look—denim skirt, boots, chambray shirt with embroidered collar and bolo tie. It wasn't going well.

"Oscar," she addressed her Abyssinian cat. "I keep trying to get this right and end up looking like the woman in the poster, *Another Victim of Santa Fe Style*. What do you think?" Oscar stretched and yawned.

"Thanks a lot."

She pulled everything off, tossed them in a heap on the bed, and dressed in her usual jeans-sweater-jacket-loafers. "I don't know if it's better but it sure feels more comfortable. Oh no!" she caught a glimpse of her clock by the bed. "I'm late."

"Come on Oscar. I'll get your breakfast."

She negotiated the ladder standing at ready in her bedroom. The house she owned was one of those "fixers" as realtors loved to call them. Actually, it had been a wreck waiting for the perfect time to collapse. She spent most of her money having the structural, wiring and plumbing repairs made. Granted, these were the most important, but they had depleted her budget. She could live with scratched hardwoods, peeling paint and the general tackiness left

4

from renters prior to the owner giving up his tax break for the more attractive occupation of former landlord. Her house was located in the coveted historical east side of Santa Fe, on a hill high enough to watch the sunsets. When she saw the deck off the living room facing west, she hadn't cared if it took the rest of her life to restore the house. At the rate it was going, it probably would.

The only completed rooms were the living and dining rooms. Both had viga ceilings made smooth by a fine craftsman of the time. Years of renting had not damaged them. Had she started in her bedroom then the last thing she looked at before she slept would have been something other than a ladder and her rehabbing tools.

Oscar's breakfast consisted of a pouring of dry cat food into an elevated ceramic bowl. His name was stenciled on the side. Oscar sniffed, whipped his tail and left the kitchen. He was clearly miffed at the slight.

"Oh, all right. You're such a prima donna. I'll get your food. Couldn't you give me a break just today? I'm not late every morning; just this one." She opened the can and poured the smelly, disgusting, brown lump onto a plate. Oscar peeked around the kitchen door and raised his nose to the aroma. Pleased, he chowed down.

"Glad you're happy. See you tonight." He ignored her as she left through the side door to the garage.

It was such a lovely day, one of those perfect Santa Fe days with a cloudless azure sky, cool morning air and the promise of a warm afternoon. Yes, this was a Mustang day. She passed on the almost mandatory—in Santa Fe—SUV for the red 1967 Mustang. Her father had collected classic cars and she caught the bug from him. When this one became available, Taylor bought it. The former owner, another woman, had cared for it painstakingly, and she carried on that tradition. The Pony had regular visits to its mechanic for tune-ups and oil changes. Taylor faithfully checked the fluid levels herself. She drove it only a few times a week, never in rain or snow. Taylor loved it almost as much as she loved Oscar.

She slid into the seat and pulled the tilt-away steering wheel into place. It had been a loaded model in its day. Hers didn't have FM radio, and she missed that, but it was a dream to drive. The Mustang was perfect for the narrow streets of the high desert town. It maneuvered well into petite spaces and around the ever present delivery vehicles which blocked traffic everywhere.

The outside of her house looked almost new. It had been painted one of the approved colors of brown. The turquoise window trim, locally referred to as Taos Blue, was just the right accent for the new mud job. Legend had it the color turquoise would ward off evil spirits, thus it was a popular color for windows in the city. The house was a single story adobe with two bedrooms. Its rounded corners reminded Taylor of a spice cookie. The front door was recessed under a covered portal with vigas protruding over the porch.

The house looked larger than it actually was because of the two-car garage. She hoped to enlarge the house in time, maybe add an office. For now, her home office claimed the spare bedroom, but something off the back of the house under the aspens would be just the thing.

Taylor had done most of the cleanup work herself spending every available hour trimming and raking. She left the ancient piñon trees with their twisted branches and tasty nuts. Several large chamisa dotted her front yard adding interesting texture and bright yellow color in the fall. A bank of lilacs clung to the steep yard along her driveway.

They had been beautiful and fragrant in summer. She wanted to add wildflowers later on, maybe next year. At present, it was as good as she could get without dipping into her shriveled bank account. She drove the car toward downtown.

Taylor hastily applied lipstick while stopped at a red light.

"Is that thing ever going to change?" Mañana, she thought. That was the way of Santa Fe. It was the very reason she'd moved here, for a slower pace. She was thrilled when the position of mystery editor at Endicott Publishing became hers. It was a brand new life, away from the pressures and hectic lifestyle in Denver; a place to start new memories.

She dazzled the folks at Endicott Publishing with her knowledge of mystery pioneers like Mary Roberts Rinehart, Agatha Christie and newer authors of the genre. She was happy to be chosen for the job. Nine years as an advertising executive, whatever that was and she had never been quite sure, had convinced them she was adept at marketing and promotions. Now, she was madly reading mysteries to reacquaint herself with the mystery world. It had been years since she had taken time for pleasure reading, having grown up on the Hardy Boys and Nancy Drew; later moving on to more grownup mystery masters.

More often, she took the scenic East Alameda Street to work but today she was traveling Palace Avenue because it was closer. She swung onto Washington where her office at Endicott Publishing resided. A glance at the Sangre de Cristo range to the northeast of the city showed the peaks clear of clouds. The mountains were breathtaking. Santa Fe was nestled at the base of the Sangre's with the Jemez Mountains to the west. The golden foliage of the aspen

7

forest covered much of the mountains at this time of year. It was a vivid contrast to the cloudless sky. Autumn had always been her favorite season, and here it meant the chile harvest. The fragrance of roasting chiles filled the air. She had to admit there really wasn't a best or most beautiful season in this region, only different and distinctively lovely each in its own way.

Endicott Publishing was a two-story building of the Territorial style. Several rows of bricks, some horizontal and others vertically placed, added a decorative edge to the flat roofline. Although it was painted brown it was different from the more traditional style of adobe architecture with its rounded edges. Here the lines were straight.

Newer buildings weren't made of real adobe bricks but standard building materials with a stucco finish giving it the adobe look. The publishing office was one of those.

Caught up in the new morning, Taylor hadn't noticed the police car until she walked from the parking lot. With all the painters working on the building the patrol car was wedged between two white vans identified as Santa Fe PaintMasters and Adobe Restoration Specialists. They had been working on the office for the past week, repairing cracks in the stucco and in general giving the place a facelift. There always seemed to be buckets, spackling compound and ladders lying around. The office staff wished they'd get on with it and finish.

During the past year her only experience with the Santa Fe PD was one of polite nods. What on earth were they doing at Endicott Publishing? Other than office equipment there wasn't much to steal. Only petty cash for coffee and doughnuts was on hand, and most employees were delinquent in their contributions. Must have been someone after computers she thought. She hoped she'd taken the time to backup her files when she left yesterday. Unfortunately, she couldn't remember.

The lobby was a warm and inviting place decorated in soft brown and accented with pale peach upholstered furniture and sky blue pillows. It and the conference room were carpeted. All the rest of the office had hardwood flooring with luxurious runners on the stairs and upper hallway.

The conference room was off the reception area. Its dark double doors were closed. Restrooms were to the left of the entry and discreetly screened by a half-wall. A large hammered tin mirror reflected each visitor as they entered the foyer.

The main staircase always caught her eyes first. It was meant to be impressive. The banister was rich dark wood elegantly curved into the lobby, but ascended to the second floor straight and wide. Art work, included O'Keeffe's, Hiatt's, Burns and West's, hung on the paneled walls here and throughout. Taylor's much loved corner was the book display at the back of the lobby. Every book released by Endicott Publishing was represented on these shelves. Their bookshelves were arranged in sections containing travel, personal transformation and regional books. Her favorite, the mysteries, were clustered center stage.

"What's going on?" she asked Candi who was answering a call. She touched her headset, spoke into the mouthpiece and punched a button on her console. The phone system had the ability to Skype, interface with her computer and control the camera and alarm system. In other words: mission control. Taylor never, ever wanted to try working that thing. She had mastered, mostly, her smart phone and that was enough for her.

"Mr. Endicott's office is locked," Candi replied with

the complete confidence in her answer as a total explanation.

"Since when did that become a crime?" Taylor nodded in the direction of the cruiser out front.

Candi, whose last name was Kane—yes, really—shrugged her shoulders, combed her fingers through her now disheveled short bleached blonde hair. She could have used Candice, but she enjoyed people's reaction to her name. The young woman was also fond of short skirts and men generally liked them on her too. In her twenties, this was her first job and she seemed born to it. Whenever there was a question of most any kind, everyone knew to ask Candi. There were few secrets, but she also knew when to be discreet. She answered another call. "One moment please."

Without wasting further time, Taylor hurried up the stairs to the second floor. Her office was the second door on the right. She dropped her purse and several manuscripts on her desk and hastened to finish her sprint down the length of the building to the last office on the left.

Several people milled around Alise's desk in front of Endicott's office. Jim Wells leaned against the wall, arms crossed, with a grin on his bearded face. Jim was a highly awarded artist now living the frustrated life of a production manager while wishing for the glory days of his college years. He could change from hilarious to caustic in a blink.

Virginia Compton, senior editor and Taylor's supervisor, wanted nothing more than to get on with her day. A meticulous person, as any good editor is, she found much serenity in one organized and well-planned day after another. Translation: boring. One could count on her to know a good book when she read it, but little occurrences such as this could put her off her feed.

The only other person there besides the police officer, was Endicott's secretary Alise. She was the newest staff member and things weren't going well. Taylor, like everyone else in the office at the time, had heard Endicott's outburst the evening prior. Endicott was hard on staff especially young women. The odd thing was he seemed to genuinely like Candi.

"So what's the deal with Endicott's office?" Taylor asked. "And why the police for a locked door?"

"Alise found the door to his office locked this morning when she attempted to leave some legal forms for his signature," Jim replied. "And she picked up a voice mail this morning inquiring about him. Apparently Preston didn't show for his Moose Lodge meeting or some such."

"That certainly sounds like reason enough to call out the law," Taylor said with sarcasm.

"Mr. Endicott has not been seen by anyone since yesterday afternoon," Virginia explained. "He had a speaking engagement at the local entrepreneurs group. I tried to reach him at home, but his housekeeper said his bed hadn't been slept in last night."

"Maybe he spent the night at someone else's house," Jim offered, barely stifling a chuckle. "He is divorced." He clearly found the entire situation amusing.

"Miss," the officer turned to Taylor. "Do you have a key to this office?"

"Well, no. Doesn't Alise?"

"I don't have one." Alise was about to cry. "Mr. Endicott didn't give me a key. It's always been open before."

"Shall I get a battering ram?" Jim raised one eyebrow in question. "The basement storeroom might reveal one."

"No," the officer said. He wasn't amused. "The building super is on his way. We'll just wait for the key."

11

"Think I'll go look at production schedules," Jim said. He ambled away in his hiking boots.

"Do you think he's all right?" Taylor asked Jim as he passed her.

"Who cares?" He smiled but a sharp edge was there.

"I know he's a jerk, but he does run the company."

"He's only running the company because he's the son of Preston, Sr., who was one heck of a guy. And, I repeat, who cares?"

Taylor returned to her office and settled in to start the day. She twisted the wand on the mini-blinds and let in the light. Her office was on the west side of the building so she enjoyed the morning light best along with the views of people coming and going to the plaza just a block away. Most afternoons she had to close her blinds to the strong sunlight. Her office was diminutive, but comfortable. The desk was a streamline affair of oak with rounded ends. There was a table to her left that held her computer and printer. The walls were white stucco with her favorite O'Keeffe, "Red Cannas" hanging on the wall opposite her. Looking at the bright flowers always gave her a lift after hours of editing or during a challenging meeting with an author or agent.

She began reading the manuscript where she left off yesterday. As she turned the last page of the chapter, Luther Jacobs, the building super, wandered down the hall jangling his keys. Curious, she followed him.

Jacobs owned and managed the building. He was never in a hurry. It had taken months to get him to paint the building even though its exterior was obviously in need of a major refurbishing.

Before Taylor could get to her door she heard the scream.

∗ ∗ ∗

Jim Wells hoped, with only a twinge of guilt, some-thing had happened to Endicott. That jerk had been a thorn in his side since Preston, Sr. stepped down and handed the company, lock, stock and coffee machine to the current Preston.

Jim's career as an award-winning book designer had all but wasted away and died since the transfer of power. Pre-viously, he had designed all covers and made most of the decisions on books from end pages to typeface. Now he was the production manager keeping minute detail of each book as it went through the publishing cycle. It was a great job for someone with a head for minutia; but a real crippler to a creative soul. But who was he kidding? He hadn't done an imaginative thing in or out of the office for years. All inspiration stopped the moment Preston Endicott, Jr. bounced him out of his upstairs office. He currently shared the basement with Donald Lovitt, the accountant and pri-mary paper-pusher for the company.

Lovitt wasn't hard to work with, but he was dull in capital letters. And he couldn't tell a book by its cover. He'd been with the company from the beginning. Old man En-dicott had just about taken him to raise, put him through school on a scholarship, gave him this job and kept him on all these years. He liked the basement, wasn't one for star-ing out of windows. His numbers kept him happy or so it seemed. Good heavens, the guy was numbing.

Maybe something had finally done in Endicott. A nice heart attack would solve a lot of problems.

Until then, Jim hated his job, and he hated the base-ment, and most of all he hated Endicott for making his life the dreary existence it had become. There had been no warning, no premonition, only utter chaos when the younger man had taken over. He never figured out the why. Maybe now he wouldn't have to. Yes, the world would be a better place without Preston Endicott, Jr.

* * *

A scream filled the corridor.

Taylor rushed into the hall and nearly collided with Jim. Alise was sitting on the floor with her back against her desk. Tears were streaming, and her hands trembled. Virginia's hand covered her open mouth. She was otherwise composed. Only Candi was missing. She was either too frightened to come upstairs or was holding down the fort.

"Who screamed?" Jim asked unnecessarily.

"Don't touch anything," the officer cautioned Jacobs who stood just inside Endicott's office. The officer pressed on Endicott's neck trying to find a pulse. It was evident even to the untrained eye the man was dead. He had collapsed forward from a sitting position across the blotter on his desk. His head was lying on one side revealing a face void of color, stricken in death. His right arm rested in a pool of vomit. An overturned cup of coffee next to his hand spread its contents on several manila envelopes. A brown stain soaked what had been a white cuff. Endicott's eyes stared. Taylor couldn't be sure if in surprise or pain.

"I can't believe it," Jim exclaimed rubbing his beard thoughtfully. "He really is dead. Justice exists."

"Jim," Taylor protested. "How can you say that? The man is dead."

Jim shrugged and left Endicott's office. Taylor could have sworn she heard him whistling as he walked away.

In the next few minutes Virginia pulled Alise to her feet, and helped her into her office. The police officer called for the coroner and homicide detectives.

Taylor waited behind Alise's desk so she could look out the window as a distraction. Outside a young couple held hands and walked along the quiet street oblivious to the drama unfolding in the office building next to them. The sky was as clear as it had been earlier, but the peace had been marred.

She looked down the staircase and saw Jim sitting in reception talking with Candi. She dabbed at her eyes with a tissue.

Jim certainly was an odd man. It puzzled her that he apparently experienced none of the feelings of shock and sadness the rest of them were feeling over the loss. Could he really be happy about Endicott's death?

* * *

As Taylor observed the world outside she remembered her first encounter with Endicott. During her employment interview Taylor thought Preston Endicott was abrupt but polite. She remembered thinking it was only a formality. Endicott seemed confident in Virginia's choice and was in a hurry to leave. As she left his office that day she turned to thank him and noticed the way he was looking at Virginia. Without knowing either of them she could only guess at the meaning, perhaps one of sadness or even regret. At any rate, it had nothing to do with her.

The ambulance arrived along with several other police officers. Taylor returned to her office. She'd allow Mr. Endicott some privacy. While she struggled to concentrate on

15

a new marketing strategy, uniformed people came and went in front of her door. At last, the body was wheeled by. She sighed and hoped the worst was over.

Everyone left early. Jim and Taylor walked along the far side of the office to the parking lot in back.

"Can you believe it?" Jim asked pointing to a ladder placed neatly on the ground against the office wall.

"What's that?"

"I think this is the first day since the painters descended that I haven't had to walk over, around or through some of their stuff."

"It's the only thing right about today," Taylor said.

"Oh come on. The world's a better place."

"Jim, dry up!" Taylor increased her pace and left Jim behind. Sometimes he could be so obnoxious.

* * *

Alise decided to stay. Whoever became the new publisher would have to be easier to work for than Endicott. She nearly quit last night after his screaming fit, but jobs were not that easy to find in Santa Fe. Fate had stepped in overnight and made it a better place to work. She picked up the outgoing mail, leafed through it and noticed Endicott's handwriting on two envelopes where he added his return address. One was his electric bill and the other was addressed to his ex-wife. She would mail them on her way home.

Chapter 2

Taylor squeezed the remote control and closed the garage door on a bad day. As she stepped into her kitchen, the Saltillo tile floor and painted sage cabinets made her wish she enjoyed cooking. Alas, she was a disastrous cook.

The room was warmed by a skylight during the day. It was the kind of room people gravitated to. When she replaced the wallpaper in the breakfast nook, it would be perfect. Currently, the walls were a mess of partially scraped paper. Maybe if she focused on one room at a time, she could get somewhere with this project. She had been dabbling and not making much progress.

Oscar met her in the living room, tail held high. He weaved his way across the hardwoods. The Abyssinian had been snoozing on the window seat next to the fireplace where he spent most of everyday. It was a perfect place to watch birds. He stretched, first into down dog and then cobra pose. Thoroughly flexed, he rubbed Taylor's leg. She picked him up.

"Hi Oscar. How was your day?"

He purred contentedly and answered with something resembling "ouw."

"I know, life is hard for a cat." She stroked his agouti fur. He closed his eyes in complete happiness.

Taylor bounced down lightly on the sofa taking Oscar with her. He curled up in her lap while she absently rubbed his ears. The soothing white stucco walls, pastel woven rugs and howling coyote folk art lightened her mood. Next to the coyote on the raised hearth sat a brightly painted barrel cactus with a tiny ladder braced against it. There was a carved rabbit in her favorite store she wanted to buy next pay day. It would make a nice addition to her growing collection.

The coyote she had purchased on a much earlier visit. They were no longer as popular. Chickens seem to have taken over. Santa Fe depended on tourism and the latest popular item was constantly evolving. Jewelry and pottery managed to stay trendy all the time.

"Let's go watch the sunset."

Oscar followed her outside onto the deck. Sunset was one of the best reasons to live in Santa Fe. This daily spectacle would make the endless months of late-night painting and cleaning, aching muscles and sore neck worth it. Oscar's fur ruffled slightly as her fingers tickled his side and he stretched to catch the last warm sunbeam of the day.

"You wouldn't believe my day." He looked up in mild interest and proceeded to catnap.

What on earth had happened to Preston? Did he have a heart attack? Taylor couldn't remember hearing any talk about possible health problems. Surely Virginia would have said something. She seemed to hover over him. How awful to die alone like that with no one to hold your hand or say goodbye. She had been unable to stop herself from glancing up as Preston's covered body was rolled by her office on a gurney. That was a memory she didn't want to keep.

Taylor returned her attention to the sunset in its final ovation. Sandia Peak in all its massive grandeur really did look like a watermelon. It was easy to understand why it had been so named. Sandia was such a charming word; much more lovely to the ears than watermelon.

"Time to eat, boy."

After tuna salad, shared with Oscar, and a glass of pinot noir, the morning tragedy was pushed to a remote area of Taylor's mind. She turned on the TV in the nook and curled up to catch the weather report, a habit developed during years of living in a capricious climate like the Midwest where she grew up. And while Denver had much lovely weather, it could snow until you had to dig out your car. Santa Fe had terrific weather. It had not been difficult getting used to it. Three hundred plus days of sunshine, cool nights and dry mountain air had an energizing effect.

The mystery manuscript she had been reading rested on the ledge with the TV. She settled back on the cushioned banco and began her nightly ritual of searching for the next great mystery. Much of her reading had to be done at home as there always seemed to be something that just had to get done at the office. It was a bit like a treasure hunt. The vast majority of manuscripts weren't what Endicott Publishing was looking for. There were no real guidelines on this. It was something they knew when they found it, something writers had suspected for years. She was finishing page sixty-two when something on the news caught her attention.

". . . breaking news. Police suspect foul play in the death of a Santa Fe publisher and CEO. Details to follow in this evolving news story."

"What!" Were they talking about Preston Endicott? There were other publishing companies in Santa Fe, but it seemed unlikely two CEOs would have died in the same day. Murder? Murder in paradise; especially her corner of paradise?

"Oscar, would you like another glass of wine?" She raised the bottle. He stared at her; his expression was one of a teetotaler condemning the ungodly. "No? Don't mind if I do."

* * *

"So they think someone killed the degenerate!"

Jim Wells punched off his home office TV with the remote. Things were finally picking up. The scotch sloshed precariously in the glass as he plopped down in his favorite chair. He swallowed it in one gulp and licked his lips to remove the last traces of his favorite brand. He poured another from the bottle on the floor.

"Here's to you Preston." Two swallows emptied the glass again. "One more ought to do it."

Memorabilia filled this room. An old wooden table burdened with books and old magazines cluttered one corner. A roll top desk sat beneath the only window. It too was a mess.

He put back another shot and reflected on the past. He'd meant to take all that stuff off the walls, but hadn't gotten around to it.

"Not healthy to dwell on ancient history, Jim ol'boy," he muttered.

But what the heck, he had won them all. Dozens of plaques, ribbons, trophies and certificates hung everywhere.

He'd been somebody back them. Reporters interviewed him, fans asked for his autograph and people paid money to hear him extol the many virtues of the fine arts. Rich cats wrote fat checks for his paintings at his one-man shows in New York City.

The money evaporated like water in the desert. He'd grown up poor without any idea of what to do with money other than spend it. Cars, clothes, women, even gambling; and don't forget booze. It became his friend. He still couldn't believe he'd lost everything; and had no one to blame but himself.

When Preston Endicott, Sr. offered him a job as art director for Endicott Publishing he swore he wouldn't bungle it again. Second chances didn't come along every day.

It had been one of his many fresh start days when he met the elder Preston. While hiking off a hangover on one glorious New Mexico day, he'd stopped to take in a vista. There among some early spring wild flowers was Preston taking pictures. He recognized the artist because he'd attended one of his shows and liked what he saw. He knew also of Wells descent and that most of it was Well's own fault. But there was a certain something about the young man, a drive and immense talent if only the self-destructive ways could be managed. Preston offered him a place in his publishing company as art director, a position which had not existed until that moment. The older man felt the time had come to design book covers in-house. An astonished Jim Wells accepted on the spot and began work the following week.

The months which followed were ones of intense creative pleasure. He began winning cover awards and national attention for the company. He dropped all his bad

21

habits, except drinking, which he controlled so as not to miss any work. For the first time in his life he experienced a contentedness and a full sense of belonging even better than his halcyon days. Unfortunately, the elder man's health became tenuous and his son stepped into his life effectively ending his second chance.

* * *

Jessica Endicott hadn't begun life as a loathsome woman, but after nine years with Preston, Jr., it was the only way to survive. Born to farming parents who barely scratched a living from the soil, little Jessica dreamed of a better life. When she was fourteen, her father left his family and life worsened.

Her mother attended beauty school on a government grant and then supported her family by working six days a week in the only salon in the small California town. Her mother didn't just become a hairdresser, she became re-nowned, even coiffing some of Hollywood's most famous heads. Jessica always looked trendy because mom kept up with the latest styles. It was one of the reasons the younger Preston noticed her that day at the University of California, Berkeley. She wasn't even a student. Because she was carry-ing a friend's books, Preston assumed incorrectly.

Crossing the campus with her friend she bumped into the young and handsome Preston. From that moment on she set her sights on becoming Mrs. Endicott, Jr.

By the time he discovered her roots he was deter-mined to stay in a relationship with her. He was rebellious and thought the best way to assert his individuality and in-dependence was to marry this girl from the wrong side of town and throw the marriage in his parents' faces.

His father, who at that time was not the mellow, kind man that Jim Wells would know, rewarded this youthful transgression by promptly cutting the purse strings. His mother didn't cope well with the estrangement and developed emotional problems. She became child-like, separated from his father, and went to live with her mother. She died a few years later of a broken heart.

He didn't let his father's withdrawal of support stop him. He worked his way through college and completed his MBA. In a few years he had become a successful businessman moving from opportunity to opportunity. It was the game that was fun. He watched trends and was always front and center for the next big moneymaking break.

However, after the newly married bliss wore off, Preston Jr. never forgave Jessica for coming into his life. He blamed her for his parent's alienation. In a short time, he grew to hate her yet refused to let her go. She pleaded for a divorce. He declined, convincing her he still cared, only to punish her again. She'd spent most of her time alone while he womanized and made business deals.

When Preston inherited Endicott Publishing she thought their lives had taken a turn for the better. The move to Santa Fe had been a good one for her. The serenity of the area transfused her and she even felt their marriage might have a chance. It was not to be, Preston didn't much like the prevailing small-city attitude, preferring the faster pace of Los Angeles. After all, Santa Fe wasn't even a major airport hub.

* * *

Jessica took a different approach. She became active in many organizations. She was soon recognized by nearly everyone in town who counted. The power and influence she derived from this gave her the courage she needed to finally divorce Preston and stick him for a more than comfortable standard of living. He owed it to her. Jessica had more than earned it.

This gave him another way to make her life wretched. He withheld payment every month forcing her to sic her attorney on him time after time. She found amusement in sending a stamped self-addressed envelope to him, the outdated tool of the publishing trade. He would not forget that she existed. But her life outside of philanthropic duties was empty and meaningless. Most of her energies were spent harassing the man who had made her life unbearable.

Standing at her dressing table brushing her bottle red hair, a relic left from her poor beginnings, she absently listened to the news. As a girl she confused flashy with rich and had never quite moved beyond that. A news break made her set down the hair brush. Was it Preston? Was he the dead CEO? She hoped so with every fiber of her being.

* * *

Donald Lovitt sat watching television in his dark living room. His mother napped in the chair next to him. She did a lot of that lately. Sometimes he wished she'd die in her sleep—better than continuing on as she was.

It seemed the police thought Endicott had been murdered. Didn't that beat all?

* * *

Virginia Compton sat in a wingback chair and stared at her TV screen. One tear ran down her cheek as she twisted a cloth handkerchief.

Chapter 3

Taylor wasn't surprised to find the police at the office again the following morning. She was somewhat surprised to see Virginia waiting in her office.

"Good morning Virginia."

"Oh." She sat in Taylor's visitor chair, chin in hand. "Good morning dear."

"I see the police are back." Taylor dropped a manuscript on her desk. "I guess it was Preston they were referring to on the news last night?"

"That's why I'm waiting for you," Virginia said. "It seems foul play is suspected. They're being closed mouthed about why."

"I can't believe Preston was…murdered." It was difficult to say it. The word carried so much finality. He wasn't only dead, but someone killed him.

"The police think so or what would be the point of all this?" Virginia absentmindedly swept the room with her arm.

Taylor sat down slowly. "Who would do something so

heinous? Surely, they don't suspect someone in the company?"

Virginia pulled a pencil from the jar on Taylor's desk. Holding it loosely in her hand she let it drop repeatedly. The eraser made a slight tapping sound each time it hit the desk.

"Probably routine. It'll all be over by lunch." She slid the pencil back into the jar and rose to leave.

"Virginia, who'll be running the company now?"

"I don't know. I hope it's not . . ."

Taylor could swear there were tears in Virginia's eyes as she left her office. It was upsetting of course, but Virginia Compton didn't strike her as the sappy type. What did she mean by her last statement? Who was it she hoped would not be running the company?

"Excuse me, I'm Detective Victor Sanchez." The detective stood in the doorway. He was handsome in a rough sort of way. Police work probably had a way of doing that. He was dressed in a dark grey suit which seemed to Taylor a bit too conservative for a detective, at least according to the mysteries she'd read.

"You're," he consulted a small note pad, "Taylor Browning?"

"Yes I am. Please come in. Would you like to sit down?"

"No ma'am, but thank you." He made some notes next to her name: auburn hair, green eyes, looker.

Taylor stood pushing back her chair. She leaned against her credenza. Sitting in the presence of this man made her uncomfortable. No reason really. He seemed a perfectly nice person. But Detective Sanchez was a man on a mission.

"I understand, Ms. Browning, you were present when the body was discovered?"

"Yes. That's right."

27

"Anyone else there?"

He knew she had been there so he must know who the others. Why was he asking something he already knew?

"Virginia Compton, Alise Wyatt, Jim Wells, Luther Jacobs, the building super. He unlocked the door." She thought a moment. "The officer and maybe Donald Lovitt. No, he might have been in the office, but I don't remember seeing him upstairs when they found Mr. Endicott. I believe Candice Kane was downstairs." Taylor used her full first name.

He nodded but did not add anything to his notebook, but a slight smile threatened.

"Do you know of any reason why someone would want to kill Preston Endicott?"

"None whatsoever."

"Is it true you have been employed here a year?"

"About, yes."

"How well do you know Jim Wells?"

"No better than anyone else. We've worked together on various books since I've been here. And we've had lunch or drinks from time to time, usually with some of the other staff."

"I gather he and Mr. Endicott did not get along?"

"Except for a few meetings, I rarely saw them together." It was almost the truth. She'd come upon them in the parking lot one day. They seemed to be in a heated argument, but stopped talking abruptly when she appeared.

"And when they were together, how did they get along?"

"Okay, I guess. Why?"

"The complete results of the autopsy may not be back for six weeks, but preliminary tests suggest that Mr. Endicott was poisoned."

"Poisoned!" Taylor exclaimed. "He really was murdered?"

"It looks that way."

"What kind of poison? How?"

"That's what I have to find out," Sanchez said. "How he ingested poison while in his office, alone, with the door locked. We're checking the coffee from his cup to see if it contained the poison."

"I don't envy you." Taylor said.

"So now you understand the seriousness of my questions. Care to add anything?"

"I guess I have to," Taylor responded. She told him about the scene she'd witnessed in the parking lot between Jim and Endicott. "I didn't hear anything so I have no idea what it was about."

Sanchez made notes: Argument, Endicott/Wells, parking lot. He was about to pose another question when Candi's voice broke in through the intercom.

"Taylor, sorry to interrupt but Dominique is on her way up."

"Oh no! Can you stop her? I'm speaking with Detective Sanchez."

"Already tried. You know Dominique."

"Thanks for the warning, Candi."

Sanchez raised his eyebrows in question but before Taylor could answer Dominique breezed through the doorway clutching her sizable purse to her chest. She nearly collided with the detective. Dominique Boucher, Endicott's best-selling mystery writer, reminded Taylor of a Bedouin because she wore layers of sweeping, billowing clothing. Quite a clothes horse and beautiful woman, Dominique could pull it off, but Taylor thought it all part of an effort to look mysterious. It worked.

"Oh well," she said in mock indignity readjusting her fedora over her sleeked back black hair. "I had no idea you were with someone." She raised one precisely shaped eyebrow at Sanchez as though skeptical about his existence.

"I believe you did, Dominique."

"You mean her?" she gestured in the general direction of downstairs. "Never could understand a word she said. Really, you should get better help."

Sanchez made another note: Who or what is she?

"Dominique," Taylor said with the last bit of her patience. "What do you want?"

"It's time for a royalty report."

Taylor glanced at Victor Sanchez with a look of apology.

Returning her attention to Dominique she said, "As I have told you before royalty statements are sent out twice a year. That will be sometime next month. If you refer to your contract—"

"You know me," Dominique interrupted. "I just get all confused when it comes to those legal things." She dismissed the contract with a wave of her hand.

"Have you read *Alone to Die* yet? You've had the manuscript for several weeks."

"Dominique, do you know that Preston died yesterday?"

Taylor knew from experience that Dominique could be quite demanding, but really.

"Yes, but I would assume business to continue as usual. It has nothing to do with me."

Taylor couldn't believe her ears. How could anyone be so self-involved?

"I need to finish my meeting with Detective Sanchez. So if you will excuse us."

"Oh. Well. Fine!" She left with garments swirling around her.

Taylor sighed. "Notice how she sucks all the energy from the room?"

Sanchez nodded in noncommittal. "Anything else?"

"I've told you all I know which is nothing."

"Vic." A uniformed officer called from the hall. "Can you get loose a minute?"

"If you think of anything else please give me a call." He handed her his card.

Taylor stared at the card in her hand while wondering just who in the company could hate Preston enough to kill him, and did they have a dislike for anyone else?

* * *

At 5:15 p.m. Taylor was on her way out when she noticed Jim lounging on one of the sofas in the lobby.

"Thought you'd never give it up," he said.

"Had a few things to finish."

"How about a drink?"

She considered what this could mean. They'd had drinks a couple of times, even lunch with some of the others. And there was that one day of second-hand shopping when she was furnishing her house. But why tonight? Why not tonight? She was overanalyzing. Maybe Jim needed to talk about it.

As they walked through the plaza, Santa Fe's heart and soul, Taylor remembered the first time she came to the City Different.

It was years ago, at least eight. She and Dave were on their first real vacation since their marriage several years

before. During the hour's drive to Santa Fe from the Albuquerque Sunport, Taylor felt herself transformed as the
landscape changed in the ebbing light.

When they floundered into the plaza while looking for
their hotel she could not believe the excitement. Tourists
hurried about trying to find the best deal with the artisans
at the Palace of the Governors before they packed and left
for the day. That was before she knew they came to the
Palace every day as they had for generations to sell pottery,
jewelry and sand paintings. Except for an occasional trip to
an Indian Pueblo, Taylor bought most of her crafts there.
Only Native American artists were allowed a special permit
to sell wares at the Palace.

* * *

The restaurant was located near the plaza. They took
the Mexican tile staircase to the second floor. Jim found an
empty table on the balcony and ordered a scotch for himself. Taylor bypassed the seventy-some flavors of margarita
for the house version. It was a cool evening; the overhead
heaters were on. Sitting there with the ristras hanging from
each end of the balcony always made her feel like a visitor
again and brought back happy thoughts. Before she lost
Dave; before her life changed.

"Heard Dominique swooped by today," Jim said.

"What?" Taylor's thoughts tumbled back into the present.

"Oh yes. Right in the middle of the detective's questions."

"Candi was upset," Jim said. "Dominique doesn't
know she exists. It's too bad we need authors in order to

publish books. Most of them are pretty difficult especially right before their book comes out. I can't remember how many times I've been hung up on or watched someone slam out of an office. I've always said we should never accept a book from an author any closer than a five-hundred-mile radius."

"I think they get caught in the system and become frustrated," Taylor said. "It's hard to understand why it takes so long to see their book in print. Print estimates, production, bar codes, ISBN numbers, Library of Congress, promotions, sales reps, and all the minute details in between failed to make sense unless you lived with it day to day."

"Doesn't make sense to me anyway," Jim said leaning back in his chair. "Publishing is a histrionic business."

"Don't forget all the contrived urgencies; when everything absolutely, positively has to get there overnight. A half-dozen book reviewers call me daily wanting a book Fed-Xed. I bet they make that request thirty times a day and never know if all the books arrive on time, if at all."

A few quiet moments followed and Taylor found herself wishing Jim would get to the point; unless, of course, the invitation should be taken at face value.

"Have you stopped painting that house of yours? Must be a lot of work."

"I've no idea why I thought I could do it all by myself. One thing's for sure; I'll only leave feet first." Taylor said and gasped. "Sorry, not quite appropriate considering recent events."

"Don't be sorry on my account. There was no love lost between me and Endicott."

"Really Jim, do you think you should be saying things like that with a police investigation going on?"

"Probably not, but it's no secret. Say, what did the good detective have to say anyway?" Jim said with excessive nonchalance.

Taylor wondered if she should tell Jim the truth and decided to punt instead.

"Not much. He asked a few questions, none of which I could answer. I guess it was routine."

"Nothing is routine with the police," Jim offered. "Routine questions from the police are like our standard contract; the worst possible deal."

The server walked by and he held up his nearly empty glass. She nodded in acknowledgement.

"What about you dear?"

"No thanks," Taylor said.

"Taylor, you remember the day you saw Endicott and me talking in the parking lot?"

"Well yes." So this was it. He was finally getting to it. Should she tell him that Sanchez knew or keep it to herself?

"So what?"

"It was nothing."

"I never said it was."

"Yes, but Sanchez might think differently."

"I felt I had to mention it," Taylor said. "He pressed for information, however slight."

"No harm done. People were standing in line to get to Endicott." He finished his drink. His glass hit the table with an exclamatory clunk.

"Time to get moving. See you in the morning."

Taylor finished her drink. She felt like a chump. Why did she tell Sanchez about Jim and Preston's squabble? Because he made her uncomfortable and she wanted to be honest. But did she have to be that forthright? Yes, chump about covered it.

* * *

Jim slapped the steering wheel of his Jeep and swore. "I'm in trouble now!"

Chapter 4

The following day found Jim Wells bent over a production schedule for an upcoming travel book. Making a schedule and trying to stick to it frustrated him at every step. Endicott Publishing was never on time with anything. Sometimes it wasn't even their fault. With so many details to coordinate with various businesses and freelancers it was a nightmare he lived every day. He'd give a lot to go back to full-time book designer. Now that was a great job. He didn't mind spending hours getting a detail right for a cover. Since Endicott had filed him away in the basement he'd considered quitting many times. For some reason he wasn't even aware, he continued the grind day after day. He looked up when he felt someone watching him.

"Jim Wells? Detective Sanchez. A word please."

Jim offered him a chair, an orange, molded plastic affair left over from the early days of Endicott Publishing. All the outdated and ugly things migrated to the basement.

Sanchez declined and continued to stand inside the door.

"You've heard this is now a murder investigation?" Sanchez asked.

"It's a small company, and of course there was that rather cryptic reference on the news last night." Jim knew he shouldn't be sarcastic but it seemed to tumble out in spite of his better judgment.

"Preliminary examination has revealed the deceased was probably poisoned. As an artist you would be familiar with toxic materials."

"Now wait a minute." Jim stood. "What are you implying?"

"Only that you might know about potentially deadly products." Sanchez held up his hand to silence the protesting Wells. "And if anything might be missing from the supplies."

"In case you haven't heard the full scoop on me, I am no longer the art director around here. I haven't touched a paintbrush in months, and wouldn't know if anything was missing from the art supplies."

"Why aren't you art director?" Sanchez's face revealed nothing.

"Endicott demoted me to production manager, that's why." He didn't flinch or mince words.

"Why were you demoted?"

"That is the question. He never shared his reasons with me."

"And even if he had you could quite easily keep them to yourself."

"Listen Sanchez, my feelings for Endicott are well-known, but I didn't kill him."

Sanchez ignored the protest. He was used to them.

"A small cut was found on Endicott's lip."

"So?"

37

"So would you have any idea how it might have happened?"

"I'm sure if the medical examiner can't figure it out, I would be no help whatever."

"You see an open cut like that would make a poison absorb much faster into the blood stream. It could have been made by the killer or Endicott may have cut himself shaving, or even sustained a paper cut."

"A paper cut," Jim said sheepishly. "Big deal. We all get those; part and parcel of the trade."

"I guess I don't have to tell you to stay in town until the investigation is over?" Sanchez didn't like Wells much. There was always one flippant type on every case. He made a note in Spanish: Wells/alec inteligente.

"Dangit, if I didn't let my passport expire," Jim said in his best red-neck imitation.

Sanchez left Jim to his production charts.

* * *

Taylor dropped her teal reading glasses on her desk. She could hear voices approaching from down the hall. Before Endicott's death she had been able to work for hours without allowing herself to become distracted. Now it seemed every minor commotion got her off track.

"A paper cut," Jim said to Virginia. "Sanchez said Endicott had a paper cut on his lip. Obviously, the ME was thorough, or doesn't have a lot to do. We get paper cuts every day. There's paper everywhere in a publishing business."

"Heard about the big meeting?" Jim burst into Taylor's office while Virginia remained in the hall looking apprehensive.

"What meeting?" Taylor asked.

"Appears the shift of power is about to be announced. Meeting's in an hour; conference room. Be there or be square," Jim said with exaggerated importance.

Taylor looked down at her jeans and sweater; not exactly appropriate attire for a major conference. Except for Virginia, who was always properly dressed for the corporate set, they were all pretty casual. It was one of the few policies Preston had allowed to remain. The elder Endicott had believed an imposed mode of dress hindered creativity. It was a belief she herself held, but it did catch one unaware at times. No matter, her sweater was a beautiful purple weave. The jeans would be under the table. She would only be listening today.

"Do we know who?"

"Nope, everyone's lips are sealed, at least those without paper cuts!" Jim laughed. Was she right in detecting a hint of hysteria?

* * *

Donald Lovitt was still shaky from the questioning with Detective Sanchez that morning. He was intimidated by authority figures. His private life was out of control and wouldn't improve until his mother was *gone*. Work wasn't much better. Sometimes he altered a few numbers just because he could. He hadn't always done it, only for the last few years when things seemed intolerable and his mother's medical costs went skyward.

Donald had been a charity case for Preston Endicott, Sr. From his earliest memory Mr. Preston, as he was instructed to address the man, had been a part of his

39

mother's life. He knew his mother was in love with him. He also knew Mr. Preston was married and this made his mother sad.

On his thirteenth birthday, while opening a gift from Endicott Sr., he asked her if she loved Endicott. She'd replied, "Of course, he's a dear friend. Look at the lovely books he gave you."

He'd watched his mother waste her life waiting for something that would never happen. That's when he decided numbers were a lot safer than people, and he had taken his first bookkeeping course. Numbers made perfect sense. They were either right or wrong—no maybes. His mother was so proud at his graduation from college, an education paid for by the only man who had ever contributed anything in his life; Endicott, Sr.

The one gentle pastime he allowed himself was horticulture. He loved flowers. He had been inspired by his mother who once had a flourishing garden. As she aged, the flowers lost some of their luster and vigor. When he established himself at Endicott Publishing, he installed a greenhouse on the south side of his mother's house. She was then able to putter inside at her own pace.

Lovitt had lived on his own for only a few months before his mother's health required him to return and care for her. She suffered from congestive heart failure and he absolutely refused to house her in a nursing home. There were still many good times for her especially in the afternoon and when she was most animated and cognizant. It made him happy to find her watering and weeding in the greenhouse when he came home. Lately however, she spent most of her time in her chair reading the same book repeatedly or watching TV, although she could no longer figure out how to change the channel.

Congestive heart failure can finish off a person in a flash or last much of a lifetime. It slowly takes away circulation and oxygen from the body including the brain. The circulation problems were bad enough. It had ended her daily walks. But the lack of oxygen to the brain caused her to forget small things or even entire days. It was a never ending frustration for both of them. He grew tired of constantly repeating answers to questions she was asking for the fourth time. He hated himself when his patience waned. He too began working in her conservatory; it was the only escape from their health-imposed house arrest.

Forcing bulbs fascinated him. The very idea that you could compel a flower to bloom in off-season went against anything he dealt with in accounting. The fragrance of spring was always present in the Lovitt house with tulips and hyacinths blooming in splendor on every available tabletop.

Lovitt quietly wrung his hands beneath the conference table awaiting the unknown as the rest of the staff filed in for the meeting.

* * *

No one was surprised to see Jessica Endicott there. Taylor had never met her but recognized the woman by the flaming red hair. Unlike her own auburn tresses, Jessica's brassy mane was hard not to notice. Even without the hair she would have been a standout anywhere. She was voluptuous in a tailored hot pink suit with a silk jewel neck blouse in turquoise. Stripper heels matched her suit. A single strand of pearls was her one concession to conservative office attire.

Several board members were present and Taylor assumed the two other people were attorneys for the firm. One, a woman dressed in a traditionalist navy suit closed the door when everyone had arrived. Why the door needed to be closed was a mystery to Taylor, there was no one on duty in the rest of the office except the voice mail. The other attorney introduced himself as Clayton Reynolds. He cleared his throat and began the meeting with several pages of document reading.

Taylor found her mind wandering because of the legal gibberish. Couldn't they just get to the point? She allowed herself to consider the horror Endicott must have felt when he realized he was sick. Did he know he had been poisoned? Did he know he was dying? It must have been frightening to be sick, alone and obviously unable to call for help. She wondered if he had been reaching for his phone when he fell over on his desk.

Reynolds finally got to something interesting. Jessica Endicott was the new owner of Endicott Publishing. Everyone was spellbound at that announcement. An audible and collective "Oh" followed.

Taylor was astounded, along with everyone else, that Jessica would be the publisher. She and Preston had been divorced for months. From what she'd heard about their relationship, it seemed poetic justice. Taylor realized she had been wrong. Someone besides Jim hated Preston. Jessica must. Would she kill to get the company?

Jessica took the podium and surveyed the stunned and waiting faces around the large table. This was the big moment. She had rehearsed many times because she wanted to get the most impact for her words.

"As new owner and CEO of Endicott Publishing it will be my first duty to inform the legal firm of Reynolds and Reynolds, hired by my ex-husband, that their services will no longer be required."

Jessica was thrilled to see the two lawyers' faces drain of color. There was even a small gasp from the usually together Virginia.

"A written notice will go out tomorrow," Jessica added.

Reynolds placed the documents he'd been reading from on the lectern, closed his briefcase with a snap and left the room without a word. His young assistant hastened to follow her employer.

"Next week I will make decisions relating to staffing," she said abruptly and promptly left the conference room leaving an aura of trepidation.

For a moment she had thought about softening the statement, but decided to enjoy these few minutes of power, something she'd always experienced from the victim's side. She cringed at the fact that she could so easily inflict it on others. She didn't intend to lay off the staff except maybe for Compton, figuring she had an affair with her ex-husband.

The meeting was adjourned.

∗ ∗ ∗

Could she be out of a job? The hard tact Jessica had chosen worried Taylor. Would her dream of living in Santa Fe be squelched so quickly? Would she be able to finish restoring her house? Her stomach twisted unpleasantly. She knew about dreams ending and how hard it was to start over.

Back in her office Taylor quickly scanned a book query. It saddened her that she was partially responsible for shattered dreams just by doing her job; in this case saying no thanks. If only all books could all be published. It didn't work that way in life and it certainly didn't work that way in the publishing business.

Whoever thought the creativity of writing could mix with the business of publishing must have been out of their mind. Publishing business; oxymoron or painful truth? Maybe both.

She added a rejection slip and was about to lick the adhesive on the envelope when horrified, she flung the offending envelope onto her desk.

"Could it be?" She hurriedly left her office.

"I'm going out for awhile Candi," she said downstairs.

"When will you be back?"

"I'm not sure. Have to go by the office supply store, and I think I'll be coming back by way of the police station."

"Okay." Candi's expression never changed. Taylor hadn't determined if she was actually smarter than all of them or kept her cards close to the vest.

At the police station she was escorted to a bull pen. Standard fare metal desks dominated the décor, if you could call it that.

"Ms. Browning," Detective Sanchez said extending his hand. "When I left you my card I never expected you to call." He grinned enjoying making her feel uncomfortable.

"Look, I feel ridiculous being here anyway," Taylor said annoyed.

"I'm sorry, Ms. Browning. It wasn't my intention to offend. Do tell me what's on your mind." His killer smile was emerging in the form of a smirk. "Sit down."

"Detective, you don't want to know everything on my

mind," she smiled sweetly. "Why don't I tell you what I've discovered?"

"Please do," Sanchez leaned back in his chair, arms behind him head. He looked dangerously close to falling over.

"In our business we get a good number of solicitations from writers hoping we will publish their books."

"Go on," he prompted.

"Oh, this can't be anything." Taylor stood to leave.

"Ms. Browning. Tell me what brought you all the way out here." This time there was no smirk, only brown eyes deep enough to drown in.

"Anyway," she continued. "Some of these inquiries include self-addressed, stamped envelopes."

"I'm not following."

"We lick the envelopes! Most of us do. Endicott was lying on a small stack of envelopes—on his desk—dead!" She slapped her hands in frustration on Sanchez' desk. He didn't appear to understand. She tried once more. "The cut on Preston's lip." Her voice rose. "The poison could have been on one of the envelopes."

Sanchez shouted to someone named Matt to get the evidence file on the Endicott case. Matt was breathing hard as he raced to Sanchez' desk and dropped the large file folder.

Taylor waited, not sure if she should be breathing. God, what if she was right? She must have licked hundreds of envelopes herself. What if there were more? Maybe the factory that made the envelopes had made a mistake. People all over the country could die. It was horrific to think about.

"Matt," Sanchez bellowed at the young man again.

"Yes sir."

"Is this all?

"Yes sir."

"Okay. Thank you." He seemed puzzled.

"What's wrong?" Taylor asked leaning over his desk.

"There are no envelopes in the file."

"But they were there. I saw them. They were next to his arm. Remember the coffee spilled on them?"

"Somehow they didn't make it to this file." Sanchez frowned.

"What does that mean?"

"It means that evidence may have been tampered with. In the meantime, no one, and I mean no one, is to lick another envelope in that office."

Taylor pulled out a dozen freshly purchased envelope moisteners from her purse and dumped them on his desk. "I've already thought of that."

This time Sanchez' smile was real and not lost on Taylor.

Chapter 5

I t was a perfect day for a funeral, a rare rainy day in Santa Fe. A downpour would be more accurate. They had slopped around the streets at the church service and were now making their way through the sodden ground of the cemetery.

Taylor held her umbrella close to her head. It was keeping only the top half of her body dry. Her skirt was soppy and she feared her low-heeled shoes would have to be thrown away. She thought of Jim and Alise back at the office, warm and dry. Alise was certain to be overwhelmed with the switchboard since Candi usually had competent command of it. Taylor winced as more water poured over the top of her shoe and seeped between her toes. Forget the shoes, she'd probably get pneumonia. She hoped the minister would make his comments mercifully short.

When she reached the blue canvas tent erected over the grave site, most of the group was there. It seemed a bit strange, considering her history with Preston, that Jessica had come. There was no outward appearance of mourning. Virginia looked sad, on the verge of tears but controlling it.

Donald was, well Donald. She would probably never really know him. He never allowed his business façade to drop. Candi was crying quietly into a well-worn tissue. Taylor handed her another. Candi seemed to get along with everyone at the office, even though no two were remotely alike. It made her a fantastic receptionist. Taylor thought she genuinely liked Preston. He'd always had a pleasant greeting for her.

There were maybe a dozen other people there, none of whom Taylor knew. Was one of them the killer?

* * *

Taylor changed clothes and shoes after the service and returned to work. She had worked late at the office many times but tonight there were many unfamiliar creaks and groans. She wanted to concentrate on the work at hand, the new mystery from Dominique. She could drive one to distraction but on the other hand she could crank out book after book and her readers loved them.

This one was a bit troubling considering what had occurred. She had only read the first few chapters, but it had already been established as a locked-room murder. Dominique hadn't written one before so Taylor decided to take it home where she could read uninterrupted.

Outside her office she heard a tapping noise. It seemed to be coming from Virginia's office. Taylor walked carefully across the floor hoping to avoid any creaking planks under the carpet. She thought she was the only one working late. Strangely, Taylor saw no light coming from under the door. A startled gasp escaped her as she stepped inside. The editor was staring out her window watching the

48

last of the sunset. A street lamp cast slips of light through the open blinds. Virginia was indulging in her nervous habit of dropping her pencil repeatedly on the desk.

"I had no idea anyone was up here. Are you all right?"

"Oh yes, dear. Just doing a little catch-up. The meeting and the funeral put me behind."

"In the dark?"

"Well no. I was doing some thinking first. Sorry if I frightened you."

"No problem. I was about to take home Dominique's new manuscript. Oddest coincidence, it's a locked-room murder."

She couldn't mistake Virginia's alarmed reaction.

"Sometimes I wonder if there is such a thing as coincidence." She left it hanging, not really a question, not quite a statement.

"I'll see you in the morning then. Perhaps we'll all feel better." She left before Virginia could respond.

Taylor had an overwhelming urge to run from the building. Instead she took one measured step after another. Succumbing to the anxiety would only blow it out of proportion. She steadied herself and her nerves by gripping the handrail firmly as she took the stairs to reception. Taylor felt as if someone was watching her and looked back up the stairs. No one was in evidence. Maybe the first floor was occupied? It was certainly full of shadows. It couldn't be more than twenty feet to the front door and yet it seemed much farther. She was relieved to be outside breathing in the piñon smoke that drifted through the evening air. This whole thing was making her a nut case.

* * *

After a hot bath that she knew would dry her skin and make her regret it, she reheated dinner. This dish was always better the second time; chicken tortilla soup, her own recipe. She shared it with Oscar. The Aby loved tortilla chips. He ate cat food, but she knew better than to deprive him of some of his favorite people food. Single cats, those who live alone with people, never quite grasp the fact they are not human. Relations flow along much more affably if the feline is allowed to feel human on a regular basis. If such expected portions are not provided, mysterious things begin to happen around the house. Drapes are found in shreds on the floor or vases that have stood for years ended up in a heap of pieces. Taylor had learned to allow Oscar his humanity. She fed him another tortilla strip and he crunched it, one happy fellow.

"You're a junk food kitty," Taylor said.

He blinked his gorgeous amber eyes as if to say, "whatever."

Taylor went back to the manuscript. At the end of the third chapter, she came straight up off the banco from her reclining position. She fingered through the next couple of chapters of Dominique's book, stopping to frantically read a paragraph here and there. The plot of *Alone to Die* could be the story of Endicott's murder. Her victim was not in publishing, but just about everything else seemed to fit: powerful man, disliked by nearly everyone, ex-wife.

"Geez, what is going on?"

Forget relaxing at home. Was Dominique somehow involved? Maybe there was no factory error in making the envelopes.

Who would be suspect? Surely each staff member would be a person of interest, but also his ex-wife, creditors, business enemies? Even an angry rejected author.

Taylor grabbed her legal pad. She made two headings: "Suspects" and "Motives."

Jessica Endicott was the first on her list. She hated her ex-husband, but Taylor didn't know the details, just that it had been a bad marriage.

Virginia Compton followed, but Taylor didn't think she was a viable suspect as she seemed to genuinely care about Endicott. But there was always the woman scorned.

Next was Donald Lovitt. Taylor didn't know him very well. He showed up at meetings and that was about it. He never attended holiday parties. But she'd heard his mother was ill.

Alise Wyatt was the most recent employee and Endicott had abused her verbally. The whole office had heard his castigations. Taylor knew nothing about her past that.

As much as she hated to add his name, Jim Wells went down next. It was obvious that he and Endicott did not like one another.

Candi Kane was the last staffer on the list. She had always seemed friendly with Endicott. Perceptions could be misleading.

Dominique Boucher had submitted a new manuscript which was hauntingly similar to Endicott's murder. On the bright side, if Dominique turned out to be the killer, she couldn't make unexpected appearances from prison.

She went back to reconsider the possibility of a rejected author. People were angry these days for all kinds of reasons. Getting rejected by a publisher could be hard to take. Most writers stop at disappointment, but one who feels particularly beat up by the world could become the next homicidal fanatic.

Even the authors they published could become quite distressed over the way the book was edited, their contract, why it took so long to publish, and the cover art. There were a myriad of steps in publishing a book that were not failsafe. And almost every author went through a phase near the end of the process where they became upset and hung up on one of the Endicott Publishing employees or slammed out of the office after airing their grievance. It was kind of like stage fright only noisier. The staff had become accustomed to this and could mostly ignore it. Usually the author would apologize later and all was mostly forgotten.

Of all the people who made her list, Taylor had to admit that Jessica Endicott had the best motive, but that didn't make her a murderer.

Jim couldn't have done it, she told herself. It was too hard to believe. He could be difficult, even combative, but surely it was just bravado. Weren't all artists insecure? Maybe she read that in one of their self-help books. Anyway the idea made her feel better.

Taylor studied her list again. Alise didn't seem too likely. She'd only been there a few days when Preston was killed. Taylor thought Virginia not the killing kind, whatever that was. Donald seemed docile and rarely spoke, and for heaven's sake, he took care of his ailing mother.

She was left with a list that told her nothing. Company outsiders might have it in for him. He was a ruthless businessman. What about Endicott Publishing board members? She didn't even know most of them. Perhaps a jealous husband had done him in? With her limited knowledge of the situation she wondered if anyone could be trusted.

Maybe the opportunity to do a little digging would present itself soon. Amateur sleuths always did a little snooping.

The thought of it made Taylor pace her warm kitchen and feel cold.

* * *

Alise was having another bad day. With the insufferable boss dead, she thought her troubles over. But with the takeover by Jessica Endicott, what would become of her? The office was buzzing with rumors. The thought of job hunting again made her want to move home with her parents. They told her she would never amount to anything and a series of short-term, no-count jobs seemed to fulfill their prophecy. With resolve she didn't have, she hoped that wouldn't be the solution.

Right now, she'd settle for finding that file. Jessica was looking for confrontation. All the furniture in Endicott's office had been removed as soon as the police released it as a crime scene. Workmen were now busy cleaning and redecorating the room. Jessica hovered around Alise's desk all morning asking for this and that. Alise thought she would scream if there was one more demand. Fortunately, Jessica's interest had turned to the new alarm system she was having installed in the building.

Jessica could be heard arguing with the foreman about the need for a separate alarm in the basement. She felt the additional alarm was necessary because of the relative ease in breaking into the basement windows. The amount of expensive art work and equipment kept there justified the expense.

But that left Jim and Donald with the responsibility of making certain the basement system was operative. Jim had complained about having to code two keypads: one at the lobby door and the other in the basement.

Victor Sanchez watched with amusement as Alise tore through drawers, searched the top of her desk and finally dumped the wastebasket. With all that was going on, she hadn't noticed him even though he was standing within inches of her desk. He cleared his throat and she nearly catapulted from her chair. On occasion, he secretly liked the power his position gave him. It could be amusing.

"You scared the nuckin' futs out of me," she gasped before recognizing the detective. "Oh sorry. I'm trying not to swear. My grandmother taught me that one."

"Looking for something?" Sanchez asked.

"Yes, but I'm sure it will turn up." Alise twisted a lock of her hair. This whole thing was making her a little spastic.

"I'd like to ask you a few questions." He waited for her to calm down.

"Sure," she tried to sound obliging but Sanchez was about the last person she wanted to talk with.

"The day of the murder did you enter Endicott's office?" he looked through the open door at what had been the publisher's office and noticed the bustle of activity.

"Not me. I don't even like to go in there now. Jessica, Mrs. Endicott, is redecorating; can't be finished soon enough for me."

Sanchez pondered a few moments how best to approach the subject of the missing mail. This only compounded Alise's agitation; she began twirling her hair again.

"Ms. Wyatt, is it within your duties as secretary, er, administrative assistant," he corrected. "Are you charged with taking the mail at the end of the day?"

"Yes, I go by the post office on my way home. Why?"

"Did you mail anything the day of Endicott's death?"

"Yes. Or at least the day after."

"How can you be sure, there was a lot of confusion?"

"Because it was weird."

"Weird?"

"My basket had two envelopes when I arrived that morning. No one did any real work that day so I was surprised by the outgoing mail. Usually, there is a lot more. Right before I left to go home I remembered the mail. By then, there were several more envelopes."

"Go on."

"I mailed them."

"Can you remember anything about the envelopes? Names? Addresses?"

"One was Mr. Endicott's PNM payment."

"His home electric bill?" Sanchez asked.

"Yes, he kept his personal checkbook in the desk. According to Virginia, uh, Compton, he had all personal statements sent here."

"Anything else?"

"His alimony payment to his ex-wife," she thought a moment. "And several large brown envelopes."

"Thank you. I may have a few more questions later."

"Oh sure," she said.

As the detective walked away Alise thought she could do without any more questions. All she did was mail a couple of letters. Big deal.

Sanchez was disappointed. It was almost a given that the evidence had been mailed. He couldn't believe it. Mailed! This was a new to him. What were the chances of getting those envelopes away from the postal service? He knew it was nil.

Chapter 6

"Candi," Taylor said. "I'm going to Taos to see Dominique. It will be late this afternoon when I get back."

Candi shook her head in disbelief as she watched Taylor leave the office. Why would anyone go out of their way to see Dominique?

Taylor turned off onto the Highway 285/84, or the Low Road to Taos, for the 90-minute drive. There was the more scenic High Road, but it was also longer. Today, she just wanted to get there.

Along the way she caught glimpses of the Rio Grande and the occasional float trip in progress.

She wasn't sure what she would say to Dominique when she got there but was determined to find out what had prompted her to write this particular mystery.

Despite some similarities to Santa Fe adobe architecture and tourist traps, Taos maintained its own personality. It seemed more rugged and conducive to its western heritage. And it had world-class ski slopes.

It was said that either you were a Santa Fe person or a

Taos person. There exists between the two cities a rivalry for tourism dollars and individuality, the sides not being quite equally divided, but then Taos is smaller. There is a snobbery to both which says each is more unique, quaint or less commercial than the other. Both had too many T-shirt stores to not be commercially oriented. And like any military city, most of which would not survive without the base, they dislike being a tourist draw, but depend on that very industry for their continued existence. Despite the yearly summer rush and the ski season that overcrowded the cities, they have desperately fought to maintain what made them different in the first place.

In Santa Fe, building ordinances were enacted that allow no new building in the downtown area be taller than the state capitol building, known locally as the Roundhouse. No one wants the dazzling vistas blocked by a skyscraper. Only approved colors of brown may be used on adobe structures such as homes and businesses to keep the architecture compatible with the natural surroundings. This also earned Santa Fe the nickname of the City Different.

Storm clouds gathered in the mountains near Taos as Taylor edged around the plaza area and turned onto a quiet street a few blocks away. The sky looked about to open but frequently it would blow over without a drop.

Dominique lived in a classic adobe house, at least it was classic on the outside. The stories about the lavish and eclectic interior were constantly being expanded. Those who had seen it left breathless, but were they rapt or aghast?

The best thing about Dominique was her books continued to backlist well, as her agent was always pointing out. Each consecutive advance had grown larger. The fortunate, and some would say unfortunate, consequence of this was Dominique remained with Endicott Publishing. The balance sheet showed she was worth it.

Taylor took the walk to her door, braced herself and knocked. After several minutes she tried the doorbell. She hoped the trip hadn't been made for nothing. She was about to leave when the door was thrown open.

"What on earth are you doing here?" Dominique was flush with irritation.

"Business," Taylor smiled sweetly.

"Can't business wait until a decent hour? I'm just out of bed. The least you could have done was call first."

"Oh, like you do when you visit us?" Taylor said kindly knowing she would pay. "Besides you look terrific. We should all crawl out of bed looking like you."

Dominique did, in fact, look her usual gorgeous self. Her makeup must be permanently applied to stay so perfect. Taylor felt plain around Dominique, though with fine alabaster skin and deep auburn hair she was quite striking without all the fussing needed to keep the temperamental author in full presentation.

Dominique ignored the remark and sucked up the compliment.

"Won't you come in?" She offered graciously

Taylor gasped in astonishment at the foyer of the house. There was nothing southwestern about the interior. The décor was eclectic art deco, except for the clothes Dominique was wearing, everything was black or white. The floor was highly polished tile, the stucco walls of the foyer and living room were high gloss white. The overstuffed furniture was striped in a satin fabric. Tables were ebony laminate with sparing amounts of knickknacks in highly polished silver from the Nambé Pueblo famous for their fine silver products.

58

There wasn't a trace of the usual Mexican tiles and hardwoods used in most of the region's houses. Instead of warm and welcoming, Dominique's home screamed, "Don't touch; don't get comfortable."

"Gosh Dominique, why do you live in the southwest?" Taylor knew she was treading on dangerous ground.

"I like the weather! No reason to be yet another southwest style casualty." Dominique said with triumph as though Taylor's reaction was exactly what she desired.

For a few moments they stood in awkward silence. "Have you eaten?" Taylor asked.

"No. Never eat in the morning."

"It is now afternoon. How about having lunch with me?"

"A salad would be fine. There's a café around the corner. The courtyard should be pleasant today."

The two made a stark contrast as they walked along Bent Street; Dominique in her flowing garb and Taylor in jacket and jeans. The locals were used to Dominique and other colorful characters, the tourists stopped and gaped. Dominique ate it up.

"Have we worn out your welcome in Taos bookstores?" Taylor asked.

"No," Dominique said. "But summer is the best time because of the tourists. Winter can be quiet."

There were several bookstores in Taos. Taylor visited those near the plaza during a signing for Dominique. One had a couple of resident cats. They spent time dozing in their beds, perfect reading companions; short on talk but loved a good head rubbing.

These bookstores had to be resourceful. Remaindered books could be found here along with the diverse books the area enjoyed. Books featuring New Mexico sold well to visitors. It had been a tough few years for these bookstores. Some long-time stores had gone out of business. Most struggled to keep their doors open.

The restaurant was in one corner of the plaza. The courtyard was enchanting with sunlight filtering through trees and around umbrellas. Late blooming flowers grew in window boxes and Mexican pots. Two musicians played folk music for the mid-day crowd.

They chose an outdoor table. Dominique ordered a salad, no dressing, and Taylor chose a veggie wrap. Taylor always puzzled about women on diets. Dry salad was completely foreign to her.

"What business?"

"Excuse me?" Taylor asked. Dominique had a staccato style of conversation.

"What was the business you came to see me about?"

"Oh, your new manuscript."

"What about it?"

"It's different. You've never written a locked-room murder before."

"I'm a writer. I can write more than one kind of book."

"But Dominique, in view of what has happened, your book could be about Endicott's death. You have the president of a small company killed in his locked office. Everybody hates him, including his employees, business associates and ex-wife. Does this sound familiar?"

"That's ridiculous! What could I possibly know about Endicott's demise? It's fiction."

Taylor couldn't tell if Dominique's exclamation had caught the attention of two businessmen at the next table or if they had been listening all along. She stole another glance. She would have sworn the table had been empty when they sat down. Was she being paranoid or had they been followed? Taylor tried to suppress the shiver she felt. This wasn't a fictional mystery. A man was dead. Maybe she should go back to the office and leave the sleuthing to the police.

"Did you hear me?" Dominique asked.

Taylor's phone made the alert sound. She pulled it out of her purse and saw a high wind warning had been posted for northern New Mexico in the evening. She hoped the return trip would not be spent fighting the wind.

"Uh, yes. Listen, I have to the back to the office."

"Without finishing your lunch?"

"I'll get it to go; I forgot an appointment. My phone reminded me," she lied. She really wanted to be away from these two guys sitting next to them. She glanced over and one met her eyes. She quickly looked down.

Her fear instinct kicked in. Taylor felt very much like she had the day in the doctor's office waiting on her husband, the day they received his diagnosis. The feeling of jeopardy was so strong that she simply could not resist it.

The walk to Dominique's house seemed much longer than it had earlier. She hesitated at the entrance to an alley. The alley was quicker than the street, but staying in plain sight seemed a better strategy. By the time she was safely inside her car she was beginning to think she'd overreacted, but the sensation had been intense.

Several miles outside of Taos she began to relax. She had exaggerated the threat. It must be the stress of the situation. Taylor felt foolish. The next thing she'd

think someone was following her. Driving began to relax her and she enjoyed the lovely countryside.

"Oh no!" Where had that thought come from? A
glance in the rearview mirror told her a white Honda
was trailing her, but at some distance.

"People on vacation." Taylor said aloud. "Seems like
every time I rent a car, it's white."

She slowed her car having inched above the speed
limit while contemplating the vehicle behind her. Unable to
resist another look, she found the Honda close enough to
see it was occupied by two men. Taylor's knuckles turned
white as she clasped the steering wheel.

"Get a grip Taylor, you've been reading too many
mysteries. Your imagination is getting out of hand." She
admonished herself.

There was a restaurant coming up in a few miles. If
she could turn off without the Honda seeing her and park
behind the building, the Mustang would be hidden from
view. As the only classic red Mustang she'd seen in Santa
Fe, it was conspicuous.

Taylor slowed and pretended to take in the scenery.
The Honda backed off. She continued to dawdle and the
white car became nearly a speck in the mirror. They didn't
appear to be interested in her. The turnoff was coming up
soon and she was taking it regardless. The curve she had
been waiting for appeared. As soon as her car was safely
around it she stepped up the speed for the short distance
to the bridge.

The Mustang was designed for acceleration, a feature
she rarely employed. She made a too sharp turn, the bridge
sat at a right angle to the highway. Her car skidded a bit,
but it also was a great car in a tight spot. She crossed the
narrow bridge over the Rio Grande to the restaurant. Be-

cause of telltale dust she edged slowly through the parked cars at the back until the building blocked the view from the highway. She left the car and watched carefully for the white car being careful to stay hidden behind the restaurant. A few seconds later the Honda zipped past the bridge on the way to Santa Fe.

What next? Go on home, return to Taos or stay put? Stay put. She preferred to stop shaking before driving again. The hostess sat her at one of the patio tables beneath the trees where she could watch the highway and enjoy the river. Taylor ordered an iced tea and willed her body to relax.

It was a charming area nestled in the trees with the river nearby. If those jerks showed up at the restaurant she would call the police. With all the diners it was unlikely anyone would try anything too diabolical.

"I hope to feel really stupid when I'm safe at home tonight," she mumbled to herself, stretched her legs and drank most of the tea at once. Ten minutes later a white Honda coming from the direction of Santa Fe crossed the bridge.

Taylor watched the car drive slowly through the dusty parking lot. There were two people inside, but she couldn't see them clearly. They were sure to see the Mustang among the other cars. Taylor pulled her phone from her purse and let her index finger hover over the 9-1-1 icon.

While she waited for the men to discover her, she watched as the hostess sat a retired couple. They were both clothed comfortably and had the air of those without a schedule. They settled in at a table on her left.

The men had ample time to locate her car. She could stand the suspense no longer. She left sufficient money for her tab and tip, and walked up the terraced slope to her car.

She might be walking into a trap.

No one was in sight. There were only about a dozen cars parked, including the Honda, but no one skulked between or under—she looked—any of the cars. Anyone observing her must have thought her daft.

Taylor eased into the driver's seat feeling like a total dolt. Obviously that nice couple on vacation was driving the suspicious car, not two dastardly criminal types. She couldn't believe how her imagination had gotten so totally out of control. Horribly embarrassed, she headed the Mustang home. At least no one would know about her rampant paranoia.

When Taylor reached the office she was too agitated to notice the company she worked for was no longer Endicott Publishing. Workmen had removed the sign during the day. The urgency she felt was so great she ran through the front door, past Candi, whose hand held a crumpled mess of phone messages, straight up the stairs to her office. She paused just long enough to find a number in her address book, and dialed with trembling fingers.

"I've got to talk with you."

Chapter 7

"Detective Sanchez for you Taylor," Candi announced the following morning.

"Thanks. Hello, this is Taylor."

"Sanchez here; got your message. Sorry I was out of town last night."

"I need to talk with you."

"I'm listening."

"Not now. I might be overheard and besides I've got a meeting in a few minutes."

"You got time during lunch? I've got a coroner to see this afternoon."

"Where?"

"You pick."

"How about the new place on Canyon Road?"

"I'll be there." The line went dead.

* * *

The conference room had the same feel as the last time everyone met, suspense crackled through the air. This would be the first meeting since the coup as Jim called it.

That morning Taylor had finally garnered the courage to wear her, by now, not so new southwest style outfit. She played with the silver belt buckle trying to make it more comfortable, and thought about removing the bolo tie before the meeting began.

"Hey Annie Oakley!" Jim plopped down beside her and pushed her chair around so he could get a better look. "Boots too." He grinned playfully knowing full well this was not the impression she wanted to make.

"Jim," she said.

"Yes darlin'," he drawled.

"Drop dead."

Jim howled with laughter. It would have put the mischievous Kokopelli to shame. He turned to Donald and asked him about two new players on the University of New Mexico basketball team.

Taylor was slightly amused, but determined not to show it. Jim could be so overbearing at times even when he meant well. She nervously twisted her rings, now on her right hand. It had been a difficult decision to remove them from her left, but she couldn't retire them completely. When she married Dave it was supposed to be forever.

Across the conference table Virginia made notes on her writing pad. She caught Taylor's eye and smiled politely.

The nervous fidgeting stopped abruptly when Jessica entered the room. She walked directly to the head of the table and placed her black briefcase on the gleaming surface. Today she wore a red suit with velvet lapels and black stilettos.

"It's so dark in here." She asked Alise to open the

heavy drapes, used mostly for Power Point presentations. Sunshine poured into the room. With the gloom dispensed, the mood seemed to lighten.

"You've probably all noticed by now that I've changed the name of the company to Piñon Publishing. I did this for a couple of reasons. I thought we all needed a fresh start, and I wanted a name that reflected the region."

Taylor liked the new name. The aroma of burning piñon was one of the things she loved about Santa Fe. It was especially fragrant after a rain when the clouds held the smoke near the rooftops.

"At this time," Jessica continued. "I do not plan any changes in staff." There was a collective sigh. "Changes may be in order at a later date, but for now I want to get a feel for the business. I, however, am not qualified to take on the duties of editor-in-chief so I have authorized a search for this position with a New York headhunter. I will fulfill the duties of chief executive officer and publisher.

"Jessica pulled out the CEO's chair which had become, sometime in the last few days, a much more feminine model. The dark leather chair had been replaced with one in a plum fabric that matched the other chairs in the room.

"Now," Jessica continued. "We will continue to publish the travel, inspirational and mystery lines that have performed so well for us in the past.

"Virginia, can I count on you for some extra help until the new editor-in-chief is found?"

Virginia looked wounded. In fact, she was the only one who had not loosened up after Jessica's announcement about staffing.

"I'm sure I can help out," she said woodenly.

"Okay Jim." She looked directly at him instead of out

the window as Endicott had done. "How are the covers coming on the new books?"

Jim perked up. Was she actually going to allow him to do what he was hired for? When he spoke it was with new respect.

"They're being done by freelancers. I'll be happy to check on their progress and supervise the final covers."

"Good." She turned to Donald.

"I'll need to see spreadsheets. Something that shows where we've been, where we are and where we are going, financially speaking."

Donald nodded and made a note.

"What about Dominique Boucher's latest book?"

"I'm doing the first edit," Taylor said.

"And what do you think?"

"It's different from her usual style, but good."

"Same protagonist?"

"Yes, but different plot." Taylor wasn't sure she wanted to divulge much about the storyline at this moment.

"How is it different?" Virginia wanted to know.

"It's a locked-room murder mystery."

"Really? How much have you read?"

"Only a few chapters."

"Who's the victim in this one?" Virginia pressed.

"A man." Taylor paused wondering how much to reveal; aware Endicott's killer could be in the room. "He's a rich and powerful man, hated by all, so there are plenty of suspects."

"How are the promotions going for the latest mystery?" Jessica asked Taylor. Fortunately Jessica didn't seem to be all that interested in Dominique's latest. Taylor was happy for the change of subject.

"Advance copies are out," Taylor said. "Still waiting on

Library Journal. Publishers Weekly liked it, but *Kirkus* had another opinion." Actually they hadn't liked it at all. To be more exact the reviewer hadn't liked the protagonist calling her "immature and sophomoric." Taylor felt that if the reviewer had been compelled to be so descriptive, the writer had struck a chord. Anyway, getting a bad review from one of the major media was always preferable to no review at all. At least they had noticed the book. She wasn't worried. The mystery booksellers she talked with regularly were telling her it would be a hit.

"Appearances?"

"We're waiting for a ship date from the printer to finalize book signings and readings. Reviewers for the finished book have been chosen. The warehouse personnel are on standby."

"Good. Okay, I think that covers it." She closed her briefcase and everyone pushed back chairs to leave.

"Virginia," Jessica said. "Would you mind staying?"

Taylor thought Virginia was going to faint. She'd never seen her react like this before. Virginia was the one who always had it together. Endicott's death must have been harder on her than anyone knew.

The clock in reception told her she'd have to hurry to make her appointment with Detective Sanchez. It was only a few minutes by car to Canyon Road, but the golden aspens had brought in another surge of tourists. She crept along the narrow one-way street of milling people, and hoped a parking spot would magically appear. Two blocks from the restaurant she parked. After ditching the bolo tie, she hurried down the street.

The charming restaurant along Canyon Road had several dining rooms with kiva fireplaces for frosty evenings. Today the windows were thrown open to catch gentle breezes. Red geraniums bloomed in the window boxes. Outdoor dining was available in summer under a portal or at umbrella tables clustered next to the coyote fence—spruce-fir latillas attached to a steel frame.

Sanchez was drinking coffee at one of the outside tables. He pulled down his sunglasses and looked at her over the rims.

"What do you like to drink?" he asked.

"Iced tea. Thank you for meeting with me," she added.

Over a delicious Cobb salad Taylor told him about her visit to Dominique, and how she had denied knowing anything about the murder even though her new book was similar. She left out the harrowing drive from Taos. That was too embarrassing and would weaken her credibility. He listened politely.

"What do you think?" she asked.

"You're telling me you think your author, Dominique, may know something about the murder? And she wrote about it?"

"Don't you think it's a bit bizarre? I mean the timing."

Taylor was regretting her impulse to talk with the detective. He was obviously going to poke holes in her story, and probably laugh at her again. Why had she felt compelled to call him? Because he was the only person she could trust. At least she was making that assumption.

"Ms. Browning," he said softly, folding his hands on the table top.

Oh no. He was going to be patronizing. That was worse than laughing outright.

"I don't think we have much to go on if you can't positively say the book is about the murder."

He had her there.

"I've obviously wasted your time." She picked up her purse to leave.

Sanchez touched her arm. "Please, finish your lunch," he said. "You haven't wasted my time. I . . ."

"Have a few more questions?" Taylor finished the sentence for him and sank back into the chair.

"Well, yes." He had the decency to look chagrined.

"These proposals you were telling me about."

"Queries. We call them queries."

"Do you keep track of them?"

"You mean do we log the queries?"

"Exactly."

"No. We do log solicited manuscripts as they come in, but not queries. We get so many of those it would be impossible to track them all. Most of them go back without being read. And no one licks the envelopes anymore."

Sanchez smiled. "So there would be no way to identify returned queries?"

"No. Why do you ask?"

"Seems the secretary, Alise, mailed several envelopes the day of Endicott's murder."

"But what would they have to do with the murder? Do you suspect a psycho author? Granted many writers have a love-hate relationship with publishers, but murder?"

"They may have been the envelopes on Endicott's desk when his body was found."

"My heavens. That would mean they were . . ."

"Moved," Sanchez said. "You're correct."

"But who moved them?"

"Another little thing I have to figure out."

"And we'll never know who sent them? Who the

killer might be?"

"We know one of the envelopes was his electric payment. We can probably rule out the electric company. The other was addressed to his ex-wife."

"Jessica?"

"The same."

"She's a suspect?"

"Among a growing number of persons of interest."

"Am I a person of interest?" Taylor wasn't sure she wanted to know, but the question floated between them.

"Let's say we are continuing to ask questions and look into the backgrounds of everyone connected to the deceased."

"Oh." She had to ask.

"Taylor," Sanchez said as he paid the check over her protests.

"One other thing. I wouldn't tell anyone else about the subject matter of that manuscript."

"I'm afraid it's too late."

"Who did you tell?"

"The entire office. We discussed it in conference this morning."

"I think you should take a few extra precautions until this is over. In case there is something to your theory."

"Like what? I don't own a bazooka or an attack dog, unless you count Oscar my cat." Despite her attempt at humor, Taylor didn't like the cold knot developing in her stomach.

"Don't talk about the manuscript anymore than you already have. If there is a murderer loose in the company you don't want to aggravate him, or her."

"Her?" Taylor asked.

"Women do kill. And poison is used more by women than men as a weapon. I'll be in touch."

He left her sitting in the Santa Fe sunshine thinking scary thoughts. Maybe he didn't think her story was entirely a paranoid delusion.

Chapter 8

The two women faced off across the conference room. Jessica, the newly empowered woman finally in control of her life and Virginia who feared she was losing control. Jessica almost felt sorry for her as she considered what to say.

Virginia Compton stood still by sheer will while she waited for whatever it was Jessica had in mind for her. She smoothed her slightly creased khaki skirt in what she hoped was a nonchalant fashion. Virginia was a nearly colorless person. To one who thought brown an exciting color the short, red suit Jessica wore was an affront. She couldn't imagine continuing to work at Piñon Publishing with Jessica at the helm. It was bad enough that the younger people dressed so casually, but to have the owner looking like a floozy was too much.

Losing this job she loved like life itself was something she didn't even dare think about. It *was* her life. Her parents were dead and with no family, the company was her family.

The search for a new editor-in-chief was a slap to her face delivered with a ferocity she couldn't understand. Virginia had felt nothing but contempt from this woman for as long as she'd known her. She would make the best possible editor-in-chief for the company and yet Jessica seemingly had not even considered her. Preston would not have approved.

"Virginia," Jessica said. "I must warn you, your position here is tenuous."

"I think you will find my performance . . ." Virginia began.

"It has nothing to do with your performance or abilities. I am in a good position to know full well your capabilities because my former husband went on about them ad nauseum."

Virginia blinked at the venomous tone.

"I want to know one thing," Jessica said. "Did you ever *sleep* with my husband?" She used the euphemism not to spare Virginia's sensibilities, but to trivialize her.

Virginia reeled at the question. How dare this woman ask her such a question? She knew for a fact that Jessica hated Preston, their marriage had been a twisted, ugly relationship which should have ended shortly after it began. And she knew, as did anyone who knew Preston, that he had many affairs. So why did his ex-wife care if she had been one? She would not dignify the question with an answer. Her association with her former employer was of no concern to his ex-wife. Virginia turned on her heel and left the room.

"If I find out you were with him, you're history!" Jessica said.

Virginia didn't hear Jessica's last rejoin. She was already rushing up the stairs.

Candi followed her with her eyes. She'd never seen Virginia move that fast.

* * *

Later that afternoon, Detective Sanchez entered the reception area.

"I'd like to see Mrs. Endicott?"

Candi glanced in the direction of the conference room. "She's working in there. I'll buzz her."

"Detective Sanchez to see you."

Jessica stared at the detective with decided irritation. The last thing she wanted to do was talk with him again. Did he never stop asking questions?

"I was hoping you'd have a few minutes."

"Very well, let's go to my office." She led the way upstairs. Sanchez couldn't help but appreciate the view.

Endicott's office had undergone a rebirth. Gone were all the dark, heavy furniture, the rug, even the pictures. The white stucco walls had been painted soft rose-beige, the hardwood floor had been sanded and lightened. Pale oak Mexican style furniture with green accents rested easily on Native American rugs. Every possible effort had been made to wipe out any trace of the former occupant. It was a beautiful room flooded with light from two large east facing balcony doors. Gauze curtains billowed delicately in the breeze. Sanchez knew it had cost a small fortune to redecorate on such short notice, but then Jessica Endicott was the benefactor of a large business inheritance. She could well afford the renovations and priority service.

Jessica crossed the room and stood behind her desk; the position of power.

"What can I do for you?" she said with barely concealed spite.

"I've talked with the coroner. I thought you'd like to know the results."

"Of course." She studied a costly manicured fingernail.

Sanchez consulted his notebook. "Preston Endicott, Jr. succumbed to a lethal poison called convallatoxin, similar to digitalis. It was somehow ingested, we think by licking it from the adhesive on an envelope because no traces of it were found in the coffee left on his desk. Since it only takes a minuscule amount of this poison to kill it could have been administered via the envelope. He may have lived as long as forty minutes. He was probably quite ill prior to his death."

The thought of Preston suffering and in pain was pleasurable to Jessica, but instead of commenting she asked, "What is convallatoxin?" She pronounced it correctly.

"It's lily of the valley; a flower."

"You're telling me my ex-husband was killed with a flower?"

Sanchez watched her reaction closely. If she was lying, she was an expert. He thought her adroit at many things.

"More likely the leaves, which are the most toxic part of the plant, were brewed like a tea and then applied to the envelope. It could have been painted on with a brush."

Jessica sat down. "That's incredible."

"There were some envelopes removed from his office on the day of the murder. Several queries apparently. Alise admitted to mailing two envelopes; his electric bill and one private letter. The queries were removed from the office without our permission or knowledge. We don't know, and probably never will know, if the larger envelopes she mailed were those on his desk."

"The personal letter was addressed to you, Mrs. Endicott. You included it for your alimony payment."

"What! You think I killed Preston?" She shoved her chair back violently.

"Detective Sanchez, it was no secret I hated my ex-husband. I hated him while we were married and I still hate him now that the debased scumbag is dead! But I didn't kill him, though I will be eternally grateful to whoever did. Anymore questions?"

"Yes. Do you still have the envelope and its contents? You should have received it by now."

"If the envelope in question is the check I received from Preston, yes I have received it. I threw the envelope in the trash."

"One last question?"

"Yes detective." Jessica clearly wanted him to leave.

"Do you have any lily of the valley growing on your property?"

"I wouldn't know. I'm not a botanist."

"Thank you Mrs. Endicott. That's all for now, but do stay in town." He made to leave but had one more thing to say.

"We'll be going through your trash."

Jessica placed both hands on her desk and leaned toward the detective. She enunciated each word with precision, "Knock. Yourself. Out."

In the hall Sanchez made a brief note: cool customer.

* * *

By late afternoon the coroner's report had spread like a mountain wildfire, thanks to Jim. Jessica had been discussing the mystery book covers with him when conversation turned to the latest news. Jim was quick to inform the rest of the staff.

"That lets me off the hook," Jim said. "I wouldn't

know a lily of the mountain, er, valley from a posy—
whatever that is."

"Don't be too sure," Taylor replied. "Even I have lily
of the valley growing on the north side of my house. Almost anyone could have access to it; it's a very common
ground cover."

"At least Sanchez and his lackeys won't be asking anymore pointed questions about art supplies. I haven't used
that stuff in months."

A few minutes later Taylor walked by Donald's office
on the way to the copy machine. She was about to say hello
when she noticed him furtively place something in a drawer. She leaned back out of sight and watched him close the
drawer, take out a handkerchief, and wipe his face.

Maybe Donald invited some investigation. He was in a
sweat about something. She could do a little checking herself. Her curiosity about Donald was too much to ignore.
She wondered momentarily about curiosity and cats. Would
Oscar advise her to mind her own business? Until the
murderer was found she would continue to be under suspicion too. If she could shorten the time, wouldn't it be
worth it? Sanchez didn't think she was in any real danger.
He asked her not to talk up the contents of Dominique's
manuscript, not get a bodyguard. She was sure his request,
that she be careful, was a placation.

It was almost four o'clock, not much point in trying to
get anymore work done. Taylor thought she'd run by Donald's house on the way home. He would be diligently
working until at least five. This might be the opportunity
she needed to learn more about the strange reclusive man.

The Lovitt's lived on the fringe of the city limits. It
was one of the few houses in this quaint neighborhood
that was not adobe. The white Victorian house stood out

among all the brown ones. It was quite captivating when viewed singly if a bit time-worn. It wore a blue metal roof and pretty lattice porch. The gardens were a riot of fading blooms. The untended flowers must have been a delight in earlier days.

Mrs. Lovitt answered the door after several minutes. She methodically struggled with the lock as though she didn't quite remember how to work it.

"Mrs. Lovitt, I'm Taylor Browning. I work with Donald. We met once at the grocery store. I was visiting a friend in the neighborhood and thought I'd say hello if I'm not interrupting."

"Yes dear. Come in." A welcome smile accentuated her liquid doe eyes which seemed to sparkle from within. Taylor followed her as Mrs. Lovitt walked stiffly to a chintz covered wingback chair.

"This room is lovely, Mrs. Lovitt." It was true even though it was shabby. Wasn't it the English who believed that until a chair or rug showed some bare threads, it wasn't finished? It was a lived-in house, a real home.

"Thank you. Please sit down." She waved to a small sofa placed squarely under the front window. The russet cushions were faded from strong sunlight.

"I noticed your flowers coming up the walk. Are you the gardener?"

"Oh yes, at least I used to be. I mostly work in my greenhouse now. The flower beds got to be more than I could take care of the last few years."

"These are beautiful." Taylor sniffed appreciatively the white narcissus growing in an antique bowl placed on the table next to her. Their fragrance filled the room.

"Would you like to see the greenhouse?"

"If you don't mind."

"This way dear."

The conservatory was small but functional. It had shades that could be drawn across the roof to protect tender growing things. It was situated off the breakfast nook which must have made it a pleasant place to eat. Blooming plants were everywhere, hanging from beams and resting in peat-filled work tables. There were bearing tomato plants and a variety of fresh herbs ready for a salad; but no lily of the valley anywhere.

"Mrs. Lovitt, this is wonderful."

"Donald brings me new plants all the time. Like the herbs. So nice to have fresh parsley."

"You must spend a lot of time working here." Taylor said.

"Not as much as before. Doctor says my heart isn't what it used to be." She tapped her chest. "Still keeps ticking though."

"Oh, look at the time." Taylor said. "I've got to be going. Thank you for showing me your plants. I hope I see you again soon. Certainly for the office Christmas party."

"That would be lovely dear."

Several pictures hung near the front door; Taylor stopped to look at them. "Is this a family portrait?"

"Yes." She pointed out herself and a much younger Donald. Her parents, brother, and two sisters were in the old photo along with their children. She mentioned each by name.

"I've always liked these old round frames," Mrs. Lovitt said. "I don't think they make them anymore."

As Taylor pulled away from the curb she felt guilty for intruding into the kind lady's life. She hoped Donald was still working. She didn't want to meet him on the street or be caught snooping. Donald seemed an okay guy. Still, everyone was under suspicion. But without lily of the valley, that seemed to eliminate him as the killer.

The oddest thing occurred to Taylor during the drive home. Everyone in the Lovitt family photo had a striking resemblance. Everyone, that is, except Donald.

Chapter 9

Hey Browning," Jim said over the phone. "That jazz trio you like so well is playing tonight at La Fonda. Why don't I pick you up and let's take a listen?"

This sounded a lot like a date. Taylor wasn't sure she wanted to. She hadn't felt comfortable dating since Dave died. The familiar ache returned as it always did when she thought of him. It amazed her that she continued to live after he was gone. On the other hand, Dave would want her to go on living and to enjoy life.

"I'd like to go." The corner turned. "Give me fifteen minutes and I'll be ready."

She changed into jeans and her most comfortable shoes. It was getting cool at night so she pulled on a long oversized burgundy sweater. She fed Oscar without the meal ritual and knew she would pay. Oscar loved his routine. After all, if it worked the first time it would continue to work: feline logic. He'd get into mischief while she was gone.

"We don't always get what we want," she told him. "I

think Mick Jagger sang that long ago." He gave her a quizzical expression as if to say, what the heck? She rubbed his now frowning head. She thought Oscar would not appreciate the Rolling Stones.

* * *

The current La Fonda was rebuilt in 1920 after the old one was torn down. It is the only hotel located on the plaza at the end of the Old Santa Fe Trail. The original inn was entrenched even before the opening of the Santa Fe Trail. The lobby became a popular watering hole where virtually every visitor in Santa Fe put in an appearance. The historical ambiance gives the feeling of walking through another time.

La Fonda's Bell Tower was a great spot to put up your feet, throw back a few and watch an incoming storm or glorious sunset. In the lobby there was a constant flow of humans into the many shops.

Taylor and Jim walked through the mingling mass of people across the work orangey-brown Mexican tile. The heavy dark beams overhead were lightened by windows surrounding the restaurant in the center of the hotel. The restaurant had originally been an interior courtyard before it was enclosed with fanciful painted windowed walls and skylights.

"Oh great, looks like the band's on a break," Jim said.

"That's okay," Taylor said. "Gives me time to start on one of their margaritas."

They settled in at a table and waited for the show to begin.

"Did you find any lily of the valley growing around your house?" Taylor teased.

"Very funny. Since I don't know what it looks like, it would be impossible for me to tell.

"I'm sure the police will check all our yards. They seem to be thorough."

"Especially good old Vic Sanchez. He really ticked me off asking questions about paint thinners and palette knives. Artists have a real killing arsenal. Course, most of us just want to be left alone to do our work. A peaceable lot, we are."

"Oh Detective Sanchez isn't so bad. He's just doing his job."

"What?" Jim almost sneered. "Do I detect an attraction to the conscientious detective? My dear Taylor, is this a grownup thing or something more akin to schoolgirl mooning?"

"Give me a break Jim. You can be so inappropriate at times."

"Sorry, wouldn't want to be inappropriate. What is it about the guy you like?"

"He seems to care about people, about his job. I think it's important to him—finding the killer."

"As far as I'm concerned the killer did the world a big favor. Jessica's going to be a lot easier to work with."

"I never had any problems with Preston."

"Given enough time, you would have."

She let the remark pass. Taylor didn't think Virginia had any problems with Preston either. She wasn't sure about anyone else, other than the revolving door of assistants.

Guests at one of the tables seemed to be having a high time. They became more vocal as minutes passed.

85

"I think they've had a few too many," Taylor nodded towards the boisterous bunch.

"Tourists," Jim said with disgust.

"Oh, they probably act the same way at home. People don't usually undergo complete personality changes because they're on vacation."

"I've lived here a lot longer than you. Trust me."

"Jim, why is it you always seem to find the worst in people?" Taylor was regretting her decision to go out with him. She was missing an evening with Oscar purring and cooing all over her. An evening at home would not have felt so confrontational.

"Just being inappropriate again," Jim said. "I'll try to watch it."

Taylor ignored him and set about to people watch. Two women talking intently in the far corner caught her attention. No, intently was not strong enough. Their conversation seemed urgent. She couldn't help but notice the familiarity of one of them. A dark woman sedately dressed, yet with a flourish. It was Dominique! Not the Dominique she knew. This Dominique lacked all the drama of dress but not of personality. Her gestures had given her away.

Dominique was trying, for once, not to be noticed. Perhaps she'd come here thinking no one who knew her would see her at a tourist hangout. Taylor did not recognize the other woman.

Before she could reflect further, a Mariachi band walked on the small stage and began playing.

"Oh no. That's not the jazz group. The paper must have been wrong," Jim said.

"I'm hardly worried about the band right now."

"That would indicate you are worried about something else. Do tell."

"Dominique's here," Taylor said above the growing ruckus.

"Where?"

"Over there. Clear at the back of the room. See her. There with that other woman."

"I think you've had too much of the green stuff. That's not Dominique, not our glitzy author."

"Watch her. You'll see I'm right."

He squinted across the room at the two women.

"Maybe it's her, but why would she be here?" He looked questioningly at Taylor.

"Can't answer that one. But I'd sure like to know. I'm going to see if I can get closer without her seeing me."

"Taylor, why don't you leave the detecting to our man Sanchez?"

The band struck up a rousing tune as Taylor headed across the crowded bar. Someone at the rowdy table yelled, "Snake dance!"

Before Taylor could cross in front of the stage, at least a dozen people from that table formed a line and began kicking and shouting in time with the music. The band members seemed surprised and then got into the spirit. It was one of those crazy moments in time when everyone went nuts at once. All around the room others were joining the line. The din was unbelievable. Things would not have gotten totally out of hand if Taylor had stayed an observer.

"Miss, another drink," a man in a business suit drunkenly mistook her for a server. She ignored him and walked on, her eyes fixed on Dominique.

"Hey!" The drunk reached for her.

Taylor walked faster. She heard the chair scrape behind her. Was the guy going to make a scene? There was no going back, but the growing snake of dancing barflies was in front of her. Was there a way out the back of the bar? She had no idea.

"Right here, young lady," a middle-aged man said breaking the chain momentarily for her.

An arm grabbed her by her wrist. She pulled away.

"Hey buddy," the bar dancer said. "She can dance if she wants to."

"How about my drink?" asked the man tugging on her arm.

Taylor wasn't too eager to see his face, but she thought it might be important to be able to identify him. He was good looking, blonde with blue eyes. A real heart-throb, but with something off-putting about him she recoiled. Some people should never drink.

"Let go of her." The dancing man broke from the line to help her.

Taylor jerked her arm and attempted to break through the widening space. The man's grip tightened until she was about to give up. Where was Jim? Couldn't he see she was in trouble? That's when things went to pot rapidly.

"Excuse me, but she's with me." Jim tapped the back of the suit.

In a split second she was free and Jim had a fist lodged in his face.

"Leave him alone!" Taylor yelled.

It fell on deaf ears. A woman screamed. The band fled the stage, instruments in hand. The snake dancers scattered. One of the revelers caught Jim under the arms as he sagged momentarily. Jim, being the peace-loving artist, was not much of a fighter. A single blow had abruptly ended his chivalrous effort to save her. Taylor looked about for something to swing and picked up a chair. She crashed it down on God's gift to women who groaned. For a moment she hoped it wouldn't hurt his face. He passed out at her feet.

The law arrived just in time to see her soon to be famous chair swing. Next thing she was watching Jim rub his face in the patrol car they shared. Her mind slipped gratefully into neutral until they were ushered into the police station about thirty minutes later.

There were questions and explanations. When everything had been resolved, or at least rationalized to everyone's satisfaction, she and Jim bumped into Victor Sanchez as they were leaving.

He stopped dead in front of them, surveyed Jim's bruised face and her disheveled clothes and flashed the boyish grin, but this time it had a devilish quality that made Taylor want to spit.

"Snake dance, huh?" he said.

"For heaven's sake Sanchez," Jim erupted. "Let's get out of here." He took Taylor's already aching wrist and nearly dragged her out bodily. Laughter exploded behind them.

After the cab ride back downtown she and Jim picked up his Jeep from the hotel garage. The drive back to her house was mostly chilly. Jim managed to moan every time he cautiously rubbed his face. Taylor thought spitefully that if he wouldn't rub it, it wouldn't hurt. He would never let her forget this. No, she was going to owe him big time.

With a sigh of relief, she stepped through her kitchen door and closed it. Her shoe squished into a puddle left just for her.

"Oscar!"

Chapter 10

Where was it? It was here when she left for lunch. Taylor had been reading Dominique's manuscript earlier and left it on her desk. She lifted their new book catalog, a pile of mail and her printout of mystery reviewers. She even looked beneath her desk, but the manuscript was gone.

Virginia was editing at her computer. Her fingers flew across the keys as she corrected, deleted and added flourishes. She had intensity when she worked that Taylor envied. It was difficult to distract Virginia while she was editing, but Taylor thought it best to do so.

"Virginia, excuse me." Virginia held up one index finger and Taylor waited while she finished the line she was working on. Virginia was an excellent editor; every writer's dream. Several authors had remarked that she made their writing better. An editor couldn't receive a higher compliment.

"Did you take Dominique's manuscript from my desk?"

"No, I've been working on this all day." She absently

stirred a cup of tea. "This must be cold by now. I'll have to brew another.

"You might check with Jessica. Although I don't think she'd take the manuscript without mentioning it."

"Okay. Thanks."

Taylor was puzzled. She left manuscripts on her desk all the time. No one bothered them. Not even a page turned. She reluctantly headed for Jessica's office. A missing manuscript could be inconvenient but it would likely turn up.

"Is she in?" Taylor asked Alise.

"Sure thing."

Taylor hesitated at the door to Jessica's office. While it had been redecorated, she thought a smudging, if not an exorcism, might be in order. There was a sensation of iniquity hanging in the air. From what she knew of Jessica and Preston's relationship it wouldn't surprise her at all if Jessica was partly responsible for some of the residual atmosphere.

"Jessica, do you have a minute?"

"Taylor, come in." She was working at her desk. Classical music came from her CD player. Jessica waved her in and tossed back her nearly neon hair in one motion. "What's up?"

"I don't want to make a big deal of this, but Dominique's manuscript is missing from my office."

"Really?" One carefully sculpted brow arched in question. "Virginia?"

"No. I already checked with her."

"No one else would have need for it?"

"I can't imagine why." Taylor said.

"Can you talk for a minute?"

"Sure." Taylor took one of the visitor chairs.

91

"At our meeting the other day you remarked that Dominique's new book was different from her others. I believe you said a locked-room murder?"

"The same."

"What exactly is it about?"

Taylor didn't think she had much choice here. After all, Jessica was the new owner of the company.

"A quick summary of the first half of the book goes like this; the powerful and much despised head of a small company is found dead in his bedroom after the locked door is broken down by police. Nearly everyone is suspected, including his ex-wife."

"I see." Jessica put down her pen and gazed out the window. "The location of the story?"

"It's southwestern. Scottsdale."

Jessica sighed slightly. "And what type of business is it?"

"An art gallery."

"I just knew you were going to say book publishing." This time the sigh was audible.

"I know. The similarity has bothered me since I began reading the thing. It would have to be a coincidence. What could Dominique possibly know about Mr. Endicott's death in advance of his murder?"

"Indeed."

Taylor left Jessica to ponder the mystery.

Candi was buzzing her as she returned to her office.

"Yes Candi?"

"Our favorite author is holding on line three." Candi could not disguise her amusement at having put Dominique on hold. Taylor grinned and reached for the phone.

"Hello Dominique. How can I help?" She tried to

sound casual and hoped Dominique would find it conta-
gious.

"Taylor we really must set up more signings. My fans
tell me on Facebook, Twitter and my author website, we
are not doing nearly enough."

A publisher's constant dilemma; how much money to
spend on promoting both book and author before profits
were eaten up? Each author deserved promotion and certainly if a book is worth publishing it should be worth
promoting. With Dominique it was a finer line. Her fans
were legion, but still, the bottom line was the bottom line.

"How about something in the area?" Taylor asked.

"I was thinking Mystery Loves Company or Powell's
Books."

Ugh. Mystery Loves Company was in Oxford, Mary-
land and Powell's was the famous bookstore in Portland,
Oregon. Both coastal. Signings at either meant airline tickets and hotel bills for Dominique.

Before she could come up with a good answer,
Dominique hurried on. "Powell's really knows how to treat
an author."

"Dominique, how about I call Tattered Cover in Denver. That's not a long drive. And then set up a couple of
signings here in Santa Fe and Taos? The tourist season is
still percolating and you're bound to attract a good crowd.
When your next book comes out we'll do another push."

"That's the best you can do?" Dominique's tone indi-
cated quite clearly what she thought of Taylor's response.

"For now Dominique, it is. With Mr. Endicott's death
we are not able to access much capital. Expenditures, except for monthly bills, needed to keep the company
running, are just out of the question until Mr. Endicott's
death and his estate are settled."

"Fine. Call me when it's set." She hung up without saying goodbye or thank you. Grrr.

Taylor heard footsteps in the hall. She watched as Victor Sanchez and two uniformed police officers walked past her office. Her pulse quickened. Something awful was about to happen; again. By the time she reached Jessica's office one cop was reading Jessica her rights, the other was clicking the cuffs in place around her wrists.

"Do you understand these rights as I have explained them?" the officer finished reading.

"Yes," she nearly hissed. "What I don't understand is why?" She glared at Sanchez who stood nearby. "I've admitted to hating the man, but I didn't kill him."

"The envelope found in your garbage was treated with the poison," Sanchez answered calmly. "You should not make any further statement without counsel."

By the time Jessica was led out, a small crowd of staff had materialized in the hallway. The office grapevine was effective. A quick headcount showed everyone but Donald and Candi were assembled. Jim seemed curious, but not overly concerned. Alise looked lightheaded. She wondered if staying had been a good idea.

Taylor nearly gasped at the look on Virginia's face. Taylor was confident that Virginia's hand was hiding a smile.

"Detective Sanchez," Taylor said. "Are you sure about this?"

"I can't really discuss the new evidence," he said. "We didn't have any choice but to arrest her."

"I don't think she did it."

"Why not?"

"Just a hunch."

"When you have more than a hunch, let me know,"

Sanchez replied. "Right now we have to book her." He hurried after the others escorting Jessica out of the building.

"Well, this development leaves a very interesting question," Jim said. "Who are we working for?"

"You look like the Cheshire cat, Virginia. Know something the rest of us don't?" Jim asked.

"I would assume it's business as usual, at least until someone tells us otherwise," Virginia replied and turned on her heel.

"So Jim, how's your face?" Taylor asked wanting to break the tension.

Jim leaned against the wall in his usual stance; legs crossed at the ankles. He touched the blue-green bruise on his cheek carefully and winced, probably for her benefit.

"Hurts like the dickens. Had to keep an ice pack on it all night."

"Must have worked; the swelling's down," Taylor tried. They had endured a myriad of remarks from their coworkers. Jim was taking it in stride. For Jim, this kind of attention was as good as any. He would milk it for all it was worth.

"Still feels swollen to me." He rubbed at his face.

"How long are you going to hold this against me?"

"Why Taylor, I wouldn't do that. What kind of guy do you think I am?"

"The kind who will never let me forget it."

"I wouldn't say never. How long do you plan to live in Santa Fe?" He chuckled as he walked down the stairs.

Since she couldn't solve the mystery of the missing manuscript, Taylor turned to her promotional list. She was choosing reviewers for their latest mystery. It was important to choose the best ones for each book. No sense sending a cozy to a reviewer who reviews police procedurals.

The ARCs, advance review copies or galleys as they referred to them, had arrived and she wanted to send them to the industry reviewers such as *Publishers Weekly* and *Kirkus*. Galleys weren't much more than a photocopy of the set type with a heavier paper binding. Some publishers could afford to make them fancier with a prototype cover. They were expensive, but you couldn't beat advance reviews. They got the word out to the booksellers and librarians who read the trade publications.

Some review publications preferred a digital ARC and she had already emailed those. But for the old school reviewer who wanted to hold a book in their hands, they still had them made.

They were also helpful in soliciting endorsements such as blurbs for the back cover. Several would be going to the best mystery bookstores for reviews in their newsletters.

Booksellers knew everything; what sold, what didn't, what their customers liked and what was trending. Taylor enjoyed talking with them. Most, although certainly running a business, had a great time. They made her job fun.

She couldn't concentrate long, however. Her thoughts soon turned back to the mystery at hand. Had Jessica really killed Preston? Jessica, like Jim, had been demonstrative about her feelings for him. Or was it a great cover? If not Jessica, who? After all, she had sent the envelope to her ex-husband.

Something nagged at her. Something that happened a few days ago, she couldn't quite grasp it. The frustration was similar to misplacing an item. You knew it was there somewhere. Hmm.

* * *

Jessica squirmed uncomfortably in the backseat of the patrol car. Preston seemed to reach out from the grave to cause her continued wretchedness. For one moment she savored how it might feel if she actually had murdered him, but she would not have used poison. Oh no. If she'd killed him it would have been very messy; a hand grenade for instance, after first tormenting him for days with his eventual demise. Never mind, she'd be out on bail by evening. She would not pay for someone else's crime, even if she would have preferred the privilege for herself.

Chapter 11

Donald Lovitt held the letter in his hand. It was from a law firm. They were going to read Endicott's will. Why he was invited, baffled him. He absently stirred his cup of tea as he speculated about who else might show. Jessica was sure to be there. Endicott's parents were dead and there had been no children produced from his marriage. His business matters had been settled and Jessica had won that round and taken over the business, but his personal estate was yet to be determined. But why was he to appear at the reading?

* * *

"Taylor," Candi said. "Detective Sanchez on four."

"Thank you." Jessica had been released on bail and was back at work. Maybe something new had surfaced.

"Taylor Browning."

"Ms. Browning. Victor Sanchez. I wonder if we could talk."

"Sure. Do you want to come by my office?" Taylor asked.

"I was thinking of something on neutral ground. Would you object to lunch at Rancho de Chimayó tomorrow?"

Oh dear. Was this the latest take on criminal inquiries?

"Is this police business?"

"Partly," Sanchez hedged. "I'd like to ask you about that little, uh, soirée the other night at La Fonda. I thought the Rancho might be more pleasant for you." He hoped she bought it. Victor found himself attracted to the lovely Ms. Browning. It must be her green eyes or maybe the spark in them when she was feeling put upon. He didn't want to commit to anything other than the case right now. It wouldn't be professional; and he realized this was on the margin.

Rancho de Chimayó was another memory filled place. But she couldn't avoid them all or there would be no point in living in Santa Fe.

"Ms. Browning, you still there?" Sanchez asked.

"Yes, I'd like to go; haven't been there since I moved to town."

"Shall I come by for you at your house?"

She gave him her address.

"Uh, I have it."

Of course he had it. The police had looked about her yard shortly after the murder, taken note of the lily of the valley growing neatly in one flower bed, and left.

"What time?" Taylor asked.

"How's eleven thirty?"

"See you then." She hung up.

* * *

99

Once off Highway 285 the pace slowed appreciably as
Victor maneuvered his car along the narrow twisting black-
top northeast of the town of Pojoaque. The low hills
pushed right up to the road in some places and trees grew
in the fences along the farms. Evidence of rain in the form
of short downpours littered the pavement where gravel
and sand had washed and remained on the road. Today the
arroyos were dry, and lined with sun-bleached rocks. No
one would suspect they could run full and overflow.

After a few miles, the farms and houses gave way to
vistas of the purple Jemez mountain range to the west and
the large open areas along the highway. Green piñon dotted
the brown land behind barbed wire fences. Chamisa
hugged the shoulder of the road. An occasional outcrop-
ping of rock formations reached heavenward as if to draw
attention to itself.

Soon the vastness gave way once again to a lovely
green valley of trees as their car descended, slowing for a
lazy cow crossing the road. The village of Chimayó, about
twenty-five miles northeast of Santa Fe, was a spiritual
place.

"Would you mind stopping at the Santuario?" Taylor
asked. "I'd like to light a candle."

"Of course not," Victor said. "It's right on the way."

Victor made the turn and parked in the tiny lot.

"I'll wait here," he said. "Take all the time you need."

Taylor purchased a votive in the gift shop, crossed the
tiny bridge that spanned a stream. The gates of the Santuario were always open and hung in disrepair. She enjoyed
the quiet peace and fragrant air of the arborvitae which
lined the walk. In the courtyard she passed several crosses
and markers.

She marveled once again at the longevity of the building itself. Built in 1814 as a private chapel, the church had survived the ravages of time and changing cultures. The walls were plaster but the ceiling was heavily timbered with vigas or beams. The elaborate altar screen or reredos was carved and painted with religious symbols. The church was a faded, but ornate; a collaboration representing both Spanish and Native styles.

Holy water was to her right as she entered the Santuario. She dipped her fingers and made the sign of the cross.

Several people were praying near the altar and she walked discreetly by so as not to disturb the worshippers. The votive slipped into a holder. Many other candles were already burning and she could feel the heat on her arm as she dipped a white taper, which served as lighter, and gently lifted the flame of another candle to hers.

"For you Dave," she whispered.

Before her emotions became too strong she left the altar and ducked into the small prayer room where the discarded crutches, canes and braces spoke for those who reported they had been cured of their maladies.

In the pocito, or little well, a child was pouring dirt from the hole in the floor into a plastic bag. The blessed soil from this tiny room was believed to have sacred healing powers. The legend also claimed the earth removed from the opening in the floor during the day, magically refilled overnight. Taylor had no way of knowing the validity of these claims, but preferred to believe them. The Santuario gave her a feeling of serenity she couldn't find anywhere else.

Outside the church Taylor saw the parish priest blessing the baby of a young couple. She stood at a distance for a moment watching. When the couple walked away she approached the priest.

"Good day," he said.

He was a small man with grey hair that glinted silver in the bright sunlight. Everything about him radiated kindliness. On impulse Taylor stopped.

"I noticed you blessing their child." She hesitated. Taylor was not Catholic and had no idea if there were rules concerning this.

"I also bless grown children," he said kindly. "Would you like to receive one?"

Taylor flushed, feeling embarrassed that she must look so needy. "Yes, please, if it's all right."

"It is always all right. What kind of blessing do you wish?"

Without hesitation she answered, "I've been a bit afraid lately."

He nodded, spoke words of safety and peace, and briefly touched her forehead. It was most quieting experience for Taylor who immediately felt lighter in spirit. She thanked the priest and joyfully walked back to Victor, who leaned against his car under the cradling arms of a large tree.

"Ready to eat?" He deliberately put a light inflection to the question. Victor knew she was widowed from his inquiries regarding the background of all the people connected with the murder victim. Was this a special place for her? People made spiritual sojourns to Chimayó for many reasons. He didn't blame them.

"Famished." Taylor said. "I wonder if their sopaipillas are still the best."

"Won't get an argument from me," Sanchez said.

The other reason to visit Chimayó was the food. The restaurant at Rancho de Chimayó was an inspiration. The Jaramillo family ran the restaurant and the bed and breakfast across the road. The food and hospitality were the reasons people came in droves. In high season, visitors came by the busload.

There were only a few parking spots available. They walked under a bright sky in no particular hurry.

The front of the 1880s adobe hacienda was brightened with red chile ristras. The strings of peppers hung beneath the scarlet metal roof. Taylor and Victor chose the shaded stone path, worn smooth by thousands of visitors. Hollow logs defined the path to the front door doing double duty as planters. Purple and pink petunia blossoms cascaded down the sides and onto the path. The Virgin Mary stood in silent stone near the entrance.

The white screen door squeaked in protest as Victor opened it for her. In contrast to the bright day, the foyer seemed unexpectedly dark. The hostess greeted them. They followed her through cozy dining rooms to the back of the former home, where the sunlight played off colorful umbrellas and table cloths. Golden aspen leaves quivered in the light breeze. Shrubs, flowers and ground covers grew from every available spot spilling over the retaining walls. The beautifully landscaped eating area provided a living backdrop for a pleasurable dining experience.

They were seated on the third level of the fully terraced backyard where the bustling wait staff, clinking silver, and animated conversations could all be savored. Victor ordered her a Chimayó cocktail, a tangy mixture of tequila and apple cider—and the restaurant's specialty. Huge sopaipillas with small bowls of honey made a great sweet tooth appetizer.

Taylor knew she wanted the chicken fajitas with pico de gallo and the best guacamole she had ever tasted. Victor quickly chose carne adovada, a warm mixture of pork and

Chimayó red chile sauce. Both plates arrived steaming and in glorious color a few minutes later. For a while they ate hungrily, and in silence, to relish each zesty bite.

"So about La Fonda," Victor broke the silence remembering his mission. "What happened?"

"I was trying to cross the bar to talk with Dominique."

"She was there? No one told me that." Sanchez obviously felt he'd not been fully informed.

"That may be because I didn't mention it." Taylor said. "I meant to but for some reason, I didn't."

"Why would she have been at a tourist spot? Was she alone?"

"I was there," Taylor said. "I live here. And no, she wasn't alone."

"Why were you there?"

"Jim and I went to listen to the jazz trio. Who never showed up, I might add."

"You and Jim?" Victor gave her a pointed look. She ignored it.

"Who was Dominique with?" He changed the subject.

"I didn't know her. At least it looked like a woman across the dimly lit bar."

"On another related subject, Dominique's manuscript disappeared from my desk the other day."

"What? Why didn't you tell me?" Sanchez leaned across the table in earnest. "You didn't think it important?" His tone was that of a parent chastising a child.

"Actually," she said, and allowed some steal to enter her voice, "I did think it important; especially after it couldn't be found. And I wonder if someone else finds it relevant in some way?"

"Tell me more about the book."

Taylor told the story once more. When she got to the locked bedroom, with the man lying dead on his bed, Victor threw up his hand in reaction.

"I can't believe you didn't tell me about this."

"Well, I'm sorry," she said scornfully, "but it seemed a bit far-fetched. I admit the plot is compelling, considering everything, but it's hard to fathom a real connection."

"Has the manuscript been unearthed?"

"No. I was going to ask Dominique for another copy."

"Do that, and make one for me. Please." He softened the last word.

After a delicious meal, their server delivered dessert to their table. The golden flan rested in a pool of luscious caramel. When Taylor tasted the smooth custard, she remembered a birthday celebration a few years earlier. Dave asked the waiter to add a candle to her flan. She dropped her spoon to the ground. As she bent to retrieve it, Victor stopped her.

"I'll ask for another," he said. "Are you okay?"

"Just a memory." Taylor touched her face and felt the flush.

"About your husband?" Victor asked kindly.

"How'd you know?" Taylor asked in surprise.

"We had to do background checks on all of you. I'm sorry about the intrusion. Sometimes I have to do things I don't like. The years bring an acquaintance with loss that most of us would rather not experience.

"You too?" Taylor's heart went out to this man who understood her anguish.

"My wife and daughter were killed by a hit-and-run driver six years ago."

"I'm so sorry." She felt as if she'd been physically punched. "What a terrible loss."

"What happened to your husband?"

"Dave died of lung cancer," she said sadly. "And no, he did not smoke!" She had grown bitter about the question people always seemed to ask.

She looked into his dark eyes and saw that he hadn't been going to ask.

"I'm sorry. It's just. . ."

"No need to apologize. People say a lot of stupid things when they try to be helpful. We want reasons for why things happen, perhaps in order to avoid the same tragedies in our own lives. Sometimes there aren't any tidy explanations."

"You know?" Taylor asked.

"Yes." He covered her hand with his.

Chapter 12

Virginia had been editing a manuscript all morning under the portal at the back of her house. She had long ago placed a table on the brick floor for this purpose. The courtyard had desert landscaping to keep down maintenance. Several glazed brown pots held red geraniums, her only accent color.

She stretched her aching back, and her gaze lifted to the Sangre de Cristo, or Blood of Christ mountains. She thought nothing was more beautiful than seeing the mountains turn deep red at sunset. All work stopped while she took a few minutes to relax and let nature do its thing.

The enclosed courtyard made her decision to buy this house a quick one. It was a sanctuary from the hectic pace her days usually demanded. A small grove of aspen, now dressed in autumn gold, formed a protective secluded space. A larger tree provided shade for much of the remaining yard. It made it hard to grow sun-loving annuals, but she didn't have time for planting flowers anyway.

Senior editor had proved to be a time consuming job. Of course she could cut back, but her work was the only important thing in her life, so she allowed it to expand into her private time. A long while ago there had been something else, a man, but the relationship did not work out. Virginia didn't know how to grieve so she worked until exhaustion came. It had become a habit.

Virginia had only known love once before, first love, the kind some people never recover from. Because of this she had carefully placed herself away from others, especially men. If she became close to anyone again, it might kill her. That was until Preston took over the publishing company. He was a dynamic person who knew his own mind and could immediately size up a situation and take command. The fact he was brutally handsome had caught Virginia unaware.

When she learned his marriage was on shaky ground she'd waited patiently, and not without encouragement from Preston. He had always been drawn to dependent women. They were easier to control. How he ended up with Jessica was beyond reasoning. She seemed his type in the beginning, but developed an independent streak as the years went by. When he tried to walk over her to get what he wanted, she wouldn't cower. This frustrated him.

Virginia stood ready at his beck and call, catering to his need to delegate nearly everything. She thrived on details where he gorged himself on the game of business. It was the dealing that made his blood race. He didn't enjoy staying after a conquest, not when there was another emerging. It was up to others to hold them together in his wake. He counted on Virginia to do that.

After a day of negotiations and drinking Preston had asked Virginia to dinner. She was flustered as a school girl. She had great expectations.

Preston in his usual debauchery managed to insult and

degrade her attentions. At the restaurant he preceded to imbibe to a point of no return, leaving her sitting in her Sunday best whimpering in disappointment. While he danced with some young thing, Virginia crept out and caught a cab home.

The following Monday morning he behaved as if nothing had happened. Virginia was never sure if he remembered being with her. She hated him for the way he treated her, but still loved him because she didn't know what else to do.

She picked up the envelope lying next to the laptop. The reading of the will was tomorrow. She was to be there. Would this be another slap to her face?

Chapter 13

A small group assembled in the office of Preston Endicott's personal attorney, Jason Lee. Endicott had always kept his personal matters with a different law firm than his businesses, which had been handled by attorneys specializing in corporate law.

The office fulfilled the expectations of most people regarding attorneys: dark paneling, plush carpeting and heavy furniture with leather upholstery. Nothing was remotely Santa Fe style except the adobe structure that housed the firm.

Donald arrived early, as was his habit, and he had been forced to wait impatiently for fifteen minutes in reception. He didn't know what to expect from today's reading. If for some reason he had inherited a monetary sum, would it be enough to help him out of the crippling debt that his mother's health had caused? He fingered the letter folded neatly in his jacket pocket. He didn't believe in luck; but if he had a rabbit's foot, he could have rubbed the fur off.

Virginia arrived next, nodded to Donald, then sat

stiffly in the unyielding leather chair. Her knees were squeezed tightly together, hands folded in her lap. She wanted to be somewhere else—anywhere—but curiosity had overcome her. Whether she was here or not, the world would soon know what Preston said about her.

In a bright teal suit, Jessica entered the law office right on time. She sat and carelessly crossed her legs. The assurance she felt surprised her. She didn't know what to expect, but since Preston had not taken the time to write her out of the business, she thought perhaps her chances of inheriting another sizable financial empire was possible. When she left this office, she might just be the richest and soon most powerful woman in Santa Fe. If only she knew who to thank for the opportunity.

A few family photos were organized at the left of his desk near Lee's phone. He could gaze at the happy family while lawyering on the phone. A large globe took up too much space in the office, forcing people to walk around it. However, it was dazzling in its craftsmanship. Each country was represented by a carved wooden piece, painted and highly lacquered.

Detective Sanchez arrived as the receptionist was escorting everyone into Lee's inner office. He sat at the back near the globe to observe. Ordinarily he didn't attend will readings but this one was different. It was a police matter and a murderer was still at large. He most definitely wanted to know the outcome of this meeting.

Jason Lee arrived ten minutes late as was his custom. It added to the illusion of attorneys being very important people especially as he walked quickly appearing to be in a hurry. He didn't particularly like the practice of law, it had been thrust upon him by his father, but he relished the misconception of his significance and authority.

He was dressed properly in a black suit. He always wore black when he read a will. He brightened it somewhat with a red regimental stripe tie against a white shirt. He rustled about his middle drawer even though he knew what he was looking for, cleared his throat and looked up at the people sitting uncomfortably; waiting.

Lee evaluated the face of each. The *grieving* ex-wife and the accountant wore expectant expressions. The drab woman seemed apprehensive. Perfect, just the effect he had hoped for. Detective Sanchez nonchalantly twirled the globe. It irritated the heck out of Lee when people did that. Except for the detective—he'd crossed paths with him before—he had the group right where he wanted them. He picked up the document he pulled from his desk and cleared his throat once more for effect.

He read through the usual boring legalese, looking up occasionally to see the detective stifle a yawn. Preston's ex-wife seemed ready to explode because of the slow pace he had set. Lee knew from Preston she was a hothead. With all that red hair flying about he wished he could witness her in action.

Lee stopped and excused himself while he took a sip from the cup on his desk. It was leftover stone cold coffee from that morning, but he knew they were all waiting for the bequests and as this was the most entertaining part he wanted to enjoy each moment.

"The bulk of the estate goes to Jessica Endicott," Lee read and then looked over his reading glasses to see the effect. Jessica appeared controlled but he thought was fighting overwhelming jubilation.

The mousy woman and the accountant—he hated accountants, never could dress right—appeared astonished and maybe wounded. They obviously hadn't anticipated this outcome. However, he'd finally gotten the attention of Detective Sanchez who was carefully watching the three individuals.

"We'll go over the estate in a private appointment," he said to Jessica. That was one appointment he might not keep waiting.

"To Donald Lovitt and his mother Dona Lovitt, who was a dear friend of my father, I leave the sum of $5,000 at my father's request."

Lovitt tried to remain perfectly still. How dare he insult him like this, to include him in his will and then leave almost nothing? He'd been with the publishing company from the get-go. Why $5,000 wouldn't even cover his mother's medical expenses. His feelings for Preston were culminating into hate. This was a joke. Preston, Sr. cared about his mother. He would have wanted her to have a comfortable retirement. Unfortunately, the elder Endicott had trusted his son to do the right thing.

"To Virginia Compton, my business right arm and good friend, I leave $500,000. She will always remain the love of my life."

Jessica gasped in anger. Virginia's hand flew to her mouth in bewilderment. Sanchez started to attention and watched the look exchanged between the two women. He couldn't see Jessica's face in its entirety, but the set of her shoulders screamed woman scorned. Virginia was speechless.

Nobody noticed Donald as he squeezed the letter in his pocket. Slowly, trying not to be heard, he wrinkled it into a wad of twisted wrath.

"That witch gets half a million dollars?" shrieked Jessica at the attorney. In a New York minute she loomed over his desk and glared at Lee. "This is an outrage!"

Her chest heaved in anger and her cleavage didn't go unnoticed by Lee.

Lee knew he should take control of the situation but he couldn't take his eyes off Jessica. Before he could contemplate her anatomy up close, she turned on Virginia.

With both hands she grabbed Virginia's shoulders and began to shake the terrified woman.

"What did he mean by *love of my life*? I told you what would happen if I found out you were having an affair with my husband," Jessica continued

"But then $500,000 will certainly lessen the blow of being fired; which you are! You've got one week to wrap things up and get out!"

Sanchez pulled Jessica off Virginia just as her hands reached her neck. Virginia brushed at her clothing as though removing frenzied debris Jessica's hands had deposited. She was plainly upset but holding onto her dignity with whatever shred of courage she retained.

"Enough," shouted Sanchez still holding Jessica at bay with one arm.

"That's it?" He nodded to Lee who barely concealed a smile.

"That's the gist."

"Mrs. Endicott," Sanchez said. "Time to go."

"Everything all right?" the woman at the front desk asked, alarmed, as Sanchez alternately pushed and pulled Jessica through the outer office.

"No problem," Sanchez growled.

Donald and Virginia gave Sanchez enough time to get Jessica out of the office, then left. When the door closed Lee leaned back in his chair, arms behind his head.

"What a hoot!" His receptionist wondered what he was laughing about.

Chapter 14

Dominique struggled out of her sports car in the bookstore parking lot where Taylor had scheduled her signing. The freshly printed copy of her manuscript was crammed in her jumbo bag. She was put out and inconvenienced that Taylor had lost her manuscript. What kind of publishing house would lose an author's work?

She hoped Taylor was right about the tourist traffic. She'd much rather be signing at a major mystery bookstore than an indie here in Santa Fe. It seemed unlikely she would make gas money back home.

Kokopelli Bookseller, located on Paseo de Peralta was a favorite in the city. Originally a home, it had once housed a restaurant and was full of paneled rooms, walls of books, sliding ladders and fireplaces. A cozy coffeehouse at the back caught the morning sun. It served soups and sandwiches made from fresh-baked bread and delectable desserts. Thursday through Saturday evenings a classical guitarist provided entertainment for cappuccino sippers in the courtyard. The store cat, End Pages, resided in what had been the living room of the house. His bed was situated comfortably near the large marble fireplace. During business hours he greeted customers from the checkout counter.

Early, Dominique breezed through the courtyard and entered by way of the coffeehouse which at this time of day was about half-full of coffee drinkers, some waiting for her, sitting at well-worn wooden tables and brightly painted chairs. She walked past the only row of booths, the highly polished bar burgeoning with muffins and croissants. She paused before the door to the kitchen. The sign tacked to the swinging door read "Employees Only." Dominique sniffed. Not one to let stupid signs or health laws stop her, she pushed open the door and entered the compact stainless steel kitchen. She dumped her purse and manuscript on the nearest counter and rummaged through a cabinet in search of tea.

"May I help you?"

Dominique whirled in surprise.

* * *

"I'll get another copy of Dominique's manuscript today," Taylor told Detective Sanchez over the phone. "She's doing a book signing at Kokopelli this afternoon. I'm going by after it's over. She's promised to bring a copy with her."

Candi buzzed her. Usually she buzzed once, but today she was insistent.

"Can you hold a moment? Candi needs to tell me something."

Taylor put Sanchez on hold and answered Candi's call.

"Taylor, Jo at Kokopelli is on line three. She's frantic. Dominique hasn't shown for her signing."

"I'll talk with her."

"Jo, this is Taylor. What's up?" Taylor listened intently for several minutes, hung up the phone and then pushed the speaker button.

"Victor," she said as she groped for her keys in her purse. "I have to run over to the bookstore. Dominique is a no-show for her signing."

"Is she normally late?" he asked.

"Only for meetings with her publisher. She's never late for her adoring public."

"Perhaps I should meet you there."

"I don't think that's necessary. She probably just had car trouble. I'll call you when I have the manuscript."

Taylor turned the Mustang onto Marcy Street and headed for Paseo de Peralta. It was a narrow twisting street at this point but widened to four lanes at Alameda. The bookstore was located near the intersection of Old Santa Fe Trail. It had one of the best breakfasts in town. Her mouth watered at the thought of the fruit frappe.

Taylor spotted Dominique's white Ferrari as she pulled into the parking lot. She was certain it was hers because of the vanity plate: MysWriter. She waved at a tan car leaving via the same entrance. It looked familiar but she was embarrassed she couldn't remember who drove it.

Dominique must have arrived while Taylor was en route. Since she was here she wanted to go in and see how the signing was going. Instead of going through the coffeehouse, Taylor took the brick path through the herb garden. The owner and head chef insisted on only the freshest herbs, fruits and vegetables for his kitchen and most were locally grown. It was a delightful tangled affair, much like an old English garden. Fruit trees grew in the courtyard and all around the house. In spring, the blooms were heady with fragrance.

Jo, the store manager, met her at the front door wringing her hands.

"Where is she? People are already here. They won't hang around all afternoon."

The bookstore was lovely. An antique desk had been set up in the large center hallway stacked high with Dominique's books. A few steps away a table was set with punch and an assortment of cookies and pastries. The tablecloth was lavender, Dominique's signature color and the imprint color on each of her books. No expense had been spared to make this an exciting event.

"But Jo." Taylor was surprised. "Her car's right out back."

"How can that be? She's not here."

"Have you looked throughout the store?" Taylor asked.

"Well no, we didn't think there was a need," Jo said pushing back a silver lock of hair. "We assumed she wasn't here." She dispatched two employees to look for the author; one to check the main floor and one upstairs. She and Taylor walked to the back.

"I'll look in the dining room and courtyard. Would you mind taking the kitchen?" Jo asked.

Taylor nodded." She had been in this kitchen before, during another signing. It was fabulous. Even a non-cooking person could admire the craftsmanship of the pine cabinets, the clean stainless counters and the high quality Viking ovens. Every imaginable size copper pan hung from the rack above the island. Only one very small pan still had its shine, the rest were tarnished with use.

The island counter was set with a porcelain tea set. Someone had prepared tea for Dominique who wouldn't be caught dead drinking punch. The tea pot was cool to the touch. A saucer held a single spoon. She lifted it and a few drops of tea ran off the spoon and stained the saucer.

A bulky handbag rested on the counter nearest the door, but no Dominique. Taylor was about to open it to check for identification, when Jo yelled from the dining room.

"She in there? No trace of her out here."

"No signs of life," Taylor started back to the door when something lying on the floor caught her eye. Upon closer examination Taylor saw it was a handle from a tea cup, part of the set. She crawled along the counter looking for the rest of the cup in the toe space. That's when she noticed a shoe sticking out behind the work counter.

She recognized the expensive Italian shoe. Dominique was fond of them.

"Oh good God!" she gasped, horrified. She reached for the counter and slowly pulled herself up. The handle dropped and shattered on the floor. Taylor moved in slow motion. She sucked in a small amount of air. Her lungs didn't seem to be working.

"Jo. In here!"

Jo burst through the door aware of the change in Taylor's voice. Taylor slumped against the island, arms outstretched, palms down, very still. She looked at Jo.

"Don't come over here. Call nine-one-one. Ask them to send Detective Sanchez and an ambulance."

"Is she?" Jo couldn't finish.

"She has to be."

Taylor could hardly bear another look. The first had been quite enough. Slowly she squatted down trying not to

119

disturb anything. She picked up Dominique's wrist and felt for a pulse. She shook her head.

The once beautiful face of Dominique was permanently contorted in fear and pain. Her staring eyes pleaded for help that would not come. On the floor near her was a shattered cup. Tea splattered the refrigerator door. Taylor backed away feeling shaky. She walked across the kitchen on wobbly legs and picked up the handbag.

Two pieces of white letter-size paper were inside the purse. The manuscript pages where 384 and 385; the last two pages of Dominique's new book. Before she could think about what that meant, Jo ushered the paramedics into the kitchen. Through the open door, Taylor saw two of Jo's employees sitting at a table in the dining room. Both were young and looked about to run. Taylor didn't blame them. Running had great appeal at the moment.

Two police officers entered with Detective Sanchez. He was all business. Taylor was so glad to see him; someone who knew what to do.

"You found the body?" he asked, now his official self.

Taylor nodded and wished for a little more Victor and less detective. She left the police to their grim chores and carried Dominique's handbag out of the kitchen where she joined Jo at a table.

By this time the police had locked down the store and were taking statements from everyone. An officer stood at both entrances turning away Dominique's fans. From the look of the steady stream of people, the signing would have been very successful. Dominique would have loved it.

"You two up to some questions?" Victor asked seating himself.

"Anything to get this over with," Jo said.

"Tell me what happened," Victor said. "And was there any suspicious people coming or going?"

"No," Jo said. "Everyone today appeared to be a customer, some are regulars, but of course, I didn't see everyone because I was working in the office."

"You didn't see Ms. Boucher come in? Had you searched for her?"

Jo told Victor what little she knew. "Since I didn't know Dominique's car was in the lot there was no reason why we would have searched the bookstore before Taylor arrived.

"Who made the tea?" Victor asked.

"No one," Jo said. "We were waiting until Dominique arrived. I set out the tea set, but hadn't made it yet."

"Someone made it," Taylor said. "But it was cold."

Sanchez looked at her, eyebrow raised. Taylor told him what she saw in the kitchen; every painful moment. He was about to close his notepad when she remembered the bag.

"This is hers." She shoved it at him.

"Where did you find it?" Victor asked.

"In the kitchen."

"And you moved it?"

Taylor realized she had unwittingly tampered with evidence.

"I'm sorry. I wasn't thinking about evidence. I thought I should keep it for her. I know. It doesn't make sense unless you're a woman." She was close to tears.

"The lab will do their best. They may be able to find some clear fingerprints. We'll need yours to rule out." She nodded.

Taylor knew he was angry. After all she had screwed up clues by handling it.

"I found these manuscript pages with it." She pushed them across the table. "It is the copy we were waiting for. There weren't any other pages."

"Looks like the killer was after the manuscript. Wonder what will happen when he, or she, realizes the pages are missing?"

Taylor wondered that too.

Chapter 15

Oscar met Taylor at the kitchen door. He had waited impatiently for several hours. While Taylor leaned against the door letting it hold her upright the Aby rubbed her legs.

"You would not believe the day I've had," she told him.

The cat meowed several times. Each successive meow became higher and more demanding. He'd had enough of this. Taylor absently rubbed the scruff of his neck. She needed to snap out of it and feed him. That's when she noticed the floor of the kitchen. It looked as if it had snowed.

"Oh no," she said resigned.

The roll of paper towels had been eviscerated. There was an ample pile of shavings on the counter. To scatter them all over the floor must have been a lot of fun. She could just see Oscar jumping and attacking enemy paper. He had a vivid imagination as he exercised his pique. This mess would likely fill her hand vac. She was obviously going to have to hide the towel roll. Oscar couldn't be trusted.

"Come on Oscar," she sighed. "Let's get you something to eat."

He followed her across the room and went through his evening ritual: he slid into the lower cabinet when she took out a can of food. He made one turn and came out the door she left open for him. Then he jumped from the floor to the counter in one perfect leap where he ate his dinner on a people plate. She had no idea why he did this every day: if it worked the first time it would work subsequent occasions?

Taylor thought this particular cat food was one of his favorites. It was certainly stinky and expensive enough to be a preferred banquet. The trouble was, his tastes changed with his cat whimsy. The solid mass, with gravy, slid out of the can whole and thumped onto the plate.

Ah, the moment of truth. Oscar licked at it hesitantly.

"Perhaps we wish a royal poison taster?"

He stopped and glared at her, as if to say, I waited all this time and you want me to eat this swill.

"You are so spoiled!" She grabbed a spoon and chopped the food into bite-size portions, rinsed the spoon of smelly cat food and dropped it in the sink. It reminded her of the spoon in the bookstore kitchen. She didn't want to relive that moment. Gratefully, Oscar began to eat.

What she needed was something soothing like tea, but right now she wanted something stronger. And besides, Taylor didn't want to think about tea. She settled for a glass of red wine.

The phone rang as she switched off the kitchen light.

"How are you?" Victor's asked; the man, not the detective.

"I'm okay."

"Sorry you found her." He quickly changed the subject. "Would you be up to a trip to Taos tomorrow?"

"I guess so." Taylor didn't want to think about going anywhere. "Why?"

"I've made arrangements with the Taos police to look at Dominique's studio. I need to get a copy of that manuscript. Can you help me locate it?"

"Sure. If there isn't a hard copy I could probably print one from her computer or save it to a thumb drive."

"Thanks Taylor. Try to get some rest."

Not once had she found a body in Denver. Not once.

Taylor and Oscar settled in on the sofa. Her fingers stroked his fur. Beginning at his ears, she scratched her way down his brown back to the tip of his tail. He buzzed comfortably on her lap as they both reclined. Taylor turned off the lamp behind her and the room was plunged into near darkness. Only the night light in the kitchen cast a pale glow into the living room. Her gaze fell on the remnants of the sunset colors through the terrace doors. Oscar was content to gaze at Taylor, his favorite subject, with sleepy eyes.

Taylor drained the last sip of wine and set the bistro glass on her coffee table. What a find it had been. Some excursions with Jim were actually pleasant, and didn't end in arrest. He found it in a bar auction right after she moved here. The low table was made of rough pine, stressed by time and use, and fit perfectly in her new life.

She carefully lifted Oscar and stretched out on the sofa. Oscar stretched and curled up beside her, settling his chin on Taylor's arm. She patted him a few times and slept.

* * *

The doorbell sent Oscar straight up out of sleep. He landed feet first with a thud on the floor. Taylor lunged, looked for a clock, and realized she'd never made it to bed.

"What time is it Oscar?"

He ignored her question while licking his way back to dignity.

Taylor looked for her phone, but it wasn't in sight.

"Guess I'll answer the door."

She was still in yesterday's rumpled clothing as she opened the door to Victor. He smiled at her disheveled appearance as she blinked at the strong morning light and pushed at her hair. Heavens, she must look a sight.

"Is it time already?" she asked.

"Afraid so. Want me to wait in the car while you get ready?"

"No, uh. Please come in. I'll be ready in a few minutes. Would you care for something to drink? I have decaf instant coffee."

Victor winced at the thought and declined. "Why don't I sit on your deck and, who is this?" He nodded at Oscar who was quietly sizing him up from the TV console a few feet away.

"Oscar, meet Victor. Victor this is Oscar. And may the best man win.

"I'm hitting the shower."

Thirty minutes later, give or take, Taylor was showered, changed and her hair mostly dry. She walked through the living room looking for casualties. Oscar wasn't known for his friendliness; especially to men he viewed as possible enemies or as contenders for his territory. He was very protective of Taylor.

She was surprised to find Victor in a deck chair talking with, or rather to, Oscar. They weren't exactly buds yet but at least they had come to a sort of détente. Oscar sat on the table next to his chair, leaning in, staring bluntly at him.

"I see the two of you are getting along."

"Oh yes," Victor said. "I like cats. Oscar's not the trusting type though. He may take a little convincing."

"He doesn't believe in face value."

"All ready?" Victor got up.

"Yes. Come on Oscar, time to come inside."

"By the way, I got a drink of water. What happened in the kitchen?"

"Gift from Oscar. Dinner was late."

"Oh?" Victor shook his head.

The drive to Taos was quiet. Taylor had never been one to wake up much before ten a.m. on weekends. That was another hour away. She was aware of the uncomfortable silence but yesterday had been a wretched day. She felt entitled to her thoughts.

When Victor pulled to the curb outside of Dominique's house, the Taos police were there. Instead of going through the residence, Victor led her around back to a guest house.

Taylor paused at the threshold. She couldn't believe her eyes. Dominique's studio was very southwest style. It was as laid back as her house was uptight. It was designed with a small kitchen lit by a skylight. She assumed there was a bath behind the kitchen. That left the living and sleeping areas next to the quiet courtyard. Dominique's large bleached pine desk sat against the only wall in the room without a window. Her computer was to one side so she could take full advantage of the French doors that looked across the courtyard bursting with flowers.

The stucco walls were white. Soft comfortable beige furniture was accented with pink pillows. The white backsplash in the kitchen was accented with a row of hand-painted tiles. A green lizard ran across each one. A thick rug in burgundy kept the feet warm. It was the most soothing place imaginable to Taylor. No wonder Dominique was, had been, such a prolific writer. She did everything possible to concoct an environment of tranquil creativity. The playfulness particularly surprised Taylor.

"Have you seen her house?"

"Yes. Very different." Victor agreed.

"She told me she hated the southwest look. Can you believe the contrast?"

"It certainly adds another dimension to an already interesting person."

"Interesting is a tame word for Dominique," Taylor said. "In fact, I've never found the precise word to describe her."

"Do you think you can find the book?" Victor reminded Taylor of their purpose.

Dominique's office was so tidy it was obvious that no manuscripts were lying about.

"May I touch things?" Taylor asked. She blushed at her blunder at the bookstore yesterday.

"Yes. It's all been dusted and searched. Our guys didn't find what we're looking for. That's why I asked you."

Taylor opened every drawer until she found Dominique's manuscript file. Each novel was carefully labeled and stored in alphabetical order. The new one was not there.

"I better try the computer." Taylor powered up the desktop model and its monitor. She knew which word processing program Dominique used. Within a few seconds she was searching the directory. She moved down the list until the last directory entry.

"I don't see it."

"Surely, she must have it somewhere," Victor said. "Perhaps on a disk?"

She glanced around the room and noticed the armoire.

"I'm assuming you already looked?" Taylor asked.

"Yes, but there was nothing obvious. Look for it hiding in plain sight."

Inside were shelves full of reference books, her published novels and what appeared to be new disks. Taylor checked each box anyway until she found the one disk hidden inside the unused supply.

"This is it." She pushed the disk into the computer drive and requested the directory.

"There," she pointed. "*Alone to Die.*" Taylor checked the printer for paper and turned it on. And then, set it for two copies and sent the document to the printer.

"Okay, just a matter of time."

While waiting for the print job, Taylor opened the lower doors of the armoire which was stuffed with paper.

"Maybe I didn't look long enough. There are dozens down here."

Each was carefully rubber banded but in no particular order. Taylor recognized Dominique's most recent published title which she helped edit. She thought these were all old versions and began replacing them on the shelf. One sheaf of paper was particularly yellow.

"This is interesting." Taylor said.

"She has someone else's manuscript."

A small wisp of dust rose when she dropped the bundle on Dominique's desk.

"Dannie Beldon?" Victor said. "Did she ever mention anyone by this name? Perhaps a friend or family member?"

"As far as I know Dominique had few friends, at least not anyone close. She never mentioned any family. Just hordes of adoring fans."

"How about a pen name?"

"We normally know when an author uses a *nom de plume*. Royalties are paid using their real name."

"Still," Victor rubbed his chin. "The initials D.B. are compelling. They're the same as Ms. Boucher's. It's very curious."

Taylor had to agree.

Chapter 16

T aylor turned the last page of Dominique's book and stared out the window of her office. The similarities were amazing; the locked room, the hated boss and death by poison. The murderer had been the man's former mistress. She didn't think Dominique had been Preston Endicott's mistress, but who knew? Had she killed him herself? Or had Dominique known his killer or her own?

Endicott wasn't one to take nonsense off anyone, including a bestselling author. Their voices had often risen to a crescendo unknown in operatic history ending only when Dominique left in a huff. Had she lost control and killed him? But if Dominique was Endicott's killer why was she also dead?

Taylor tried to remember if there had been any lily of the valley growing at Dominique's house, but could not recall. One thing was evident from this investigation, the ground cover grew virtually everywhere. Even if it was not grown by the killer, access was easy.

"Really Taylor, you should be more careful. Don't you know thinking wears out the brain?"

Jim leaned against her doorway, arms crossed. He had that grin on his face; the one that always meant trouble. She thought he'd forgiven her the incident at La Fonda. He seemed his old playful self again.

"What are you doing up here?" Taylor teased, knowing full well how much he wanted to make the move back upstairs.

"No one to talk with." He rubbed his short beard absently.

"Donald won't talk to you?"

"His door is closed most of the time. He mumbles something about quarterly reports, and then slinks off into the depths of his office."

"Need something to do, Jim?" Jessica asked as she walked by.

"Just on my way back downstairs," Jim said. "What's she in a mood about?"

He winked conspiratorially at Taylor and fled down the hall.

Taylor wondered too. Ever since the reading of Endicott's will Jessica had been unpleasant and prone to short but nasty eruptions. Virginia was very quiet, even more so than usual. She covered whatever was bothering her with more and more work.

The ruckus next door stopped all questions before any answers could form.

"I want you out of here by five o'clock today," Jessica was screaming in Virginia's office. Taylor could not hear Virginia's reply. Her own hearing, impaired from all the blood suddenly rushing through her head. Almost every day something happened to cause a surge of anxiety in the office.

Jim had retraced his steps and crept back into her office.

"What's going on?" he mouthed and pointed to the wall she shared with Virginia's office.

Taylor rubbed her head. It was beginning to hurt. Next door something crashed.

"No, I'm not kidding. I fired you at the law office. I meant it. You obviously had an affair with Preston."

"No." Virginia said it loud enough to be heard but it didn't reach the level of Jessica's voice. "That's not true."

"Don't give me that drivel. You were there. You heard the attorney read his will. If you weren't having an affair with him, what did he mean by 'love of my life'?"

Jim raised his eyebrows and whistled softly.

"I don't know what it meant. We had dinner. Once. Nothing else happened."

"I don't believe you," Jessica spat. "I gave you one week to wrap things up. Now take your things and go!" She slammed Virginia's door. Something fell with the sound of breaking glass. A few moments later Jessica's office door thudded.

Taylor and Jim exchanged glances. She let out her breath.

"I'm going to check on Virginia," Jim said.

"Wait. I'll come with you."

Jim knocked softly on Virginia's door and slowly opened it.

"Are you all right?" he asked.

Virginia sat at her desk in shock. Her face was flushed and her expression was one of sadness. She didn't like yelling. Nor did she ever stoop to such shenanigans. From what had transpired of late, Taylor thought maybe Jessica loved the adrenalin high she got from becoming upset. She hoped it was a phase.

The editor shut down her computer, removed the CD

and placed it on her desk pad. She pulled open the bottom drawer of the elegant walnut desk and took out her purse, appointment book and walked quickly out of her office. She left without a word.

"Virginia," Taylor tried, but had no clue what to say. She didn't have to find the words. Virginia's head disappeared below the stairs.

"I can't believe it," Jim said. "She's been here forever."

"How can Jessica do that? I simply cannot fathom Virginia, of all people, had an affair with Preston."

And like the mind sometimes does, a piece fell in place. She flew back in time to her interview for this job and remembered the look that passed between Preston and Virginia. Maybe it hadn't been sadness or regret; maybe it had been quiet passion.

Was Virginia a jilted lover? Taylor was having a hard time processing it, but that red flag waved in her mind. Virginia drank tea, she was a connoisseur, buying loose tea and then packing it in her own tea bags. Victor told her the lily of the valley could have been brewed like tea, and applied to the envelope's adhesive. Could she have both loved him and killed him?

"I think I'll get back to the dungeon before I get sacked," Jim said.

She had forgotten he was there. Taylor watched Jim clomp away in his boots. And to think she had once been suspicious of Jim. Should she tell Victor about this? She didn't want the wrong person arrested; again. Taylor knew only one thing. It was time for a hot bath. She needed to think.

Chapter 17

Oscar batted at the bubbles floating in Taylor's tub. He loved to live on the edge; the edge of the tub. Many times he had fallen through the fragile froth into the water. He climbed out quickly enough, scrambling up and over the slippery porcelain. Getting wet didn't stop Oscar from trying again. Abyssinians liked water she had read. Oscar sure seemed to enjoy playing with it as if it were a catnip toy with a bite.

Taylor dropped wads of bubbles on his brown fur creating small dinosaur ridges down his back, an odd but harmless childish thing. He seemed to enjoy the attention until the bubbles dissolved leaving wet spots in his fur that he then had to lick dry.

"Oscar you have the prettiest fur." The agouti fur of Abyssinians looks much like that of squirrels and rabbits. With further breeding they now came in nearly ten colors like ruddy, red, blue and cream. All retained the agouti fur and expressive clown markings. Oscar was a ruddy; the original.

He cocked his head to one side as though accepting

the compliment. It seemed a human thing to do and being an only kitty, he'd picked up more human traits than a cat with feline buddies might. Taylor had friends who swore their oldest cat never purred until they added a kitten to the family. Only then did he grasp he wasn't a person; a very sad insight for that particular cat, but he had learned to purr.

Something about Oscar's fur was puzzling her. His tan chest reminded her of something else.

"Yes!" She slapped the water startling Oscar who leapt to the bathroom rug, and then began to lick. The car driving out of the parking lot at the bookstore had been tan. It looked familiar to her and she had waved at the driver.

Who did she know who drove a tan car? Who was it she had teased about driving a house? Virginia! She remembered black clothing. It seemed the person had been wearing black, certainly not Virginia's color. Taylor couldn't remember ever seeing her in black. She sunk under the water with relief. It couldn't have been Virginia. Unless, of course, she had been disguised, but why on earth would she do that?

* * *

Overnight a new stack of manuscripts appeared in Taylor's inbox. She sighed as she recalled yesterday's events ending with Virginia's dismissal. Now it looked like Taylor would have to assume all or most of Virginia's work in addition to her own. The office was no place for petty personal differences. This simply was not good for the company. She missed her already and not just because she would be doing more work. Taylor liked Virginia and admired her abilities with a blue pencil, the time-honored way to edit a manuscript. Maybe Jim was in a better place since Jessica had taken over, but Taylor wasn't so sure about the rest of the staff.

While pondering her fate, Candi's lyrical voice announced that Ruth Standish waited to see her.

"Oh no," Taylor whispered. Now she had to deal with Dominique's agent of all people. Ruth was a perfect match for Dominique. To put it succinctly, they understood one another. They were two peas in the ol' pod. Egad, this had to be trouble and Virginia wasn't here to work her magic. Virginia was the only person who could calm Ruth. Taylor thought Virginia's martyr personality worked to make Ruth feel in control. Unfortunately, Taylor didn't know how to fake the servile approach.

Ruth was the very definition of battleaxe. She was a fearsome, domineering combative woman of about fifty; short, smartly cut blonde hair and not a wrinkle to be seen. Jim was sure she'd undergone plastic surgery but also admitted that, like Dominique, she never had any pent-up emotions so possibly no lines had formed.

Why was absolutely everybody in this business weird? Taylor had noticed from her first day at the publishing house that virtually everyone was at least off-beat, if not downright eccentric. However, that did leave room for Taylor. She considered herself a bit Bohemian, but in the most becoming way, naturally. Not everyone could be in sales or service. Everyone has different strengths and talents.

She swallowed and asked Candi to send her up.

"Well, this is a fine mess," Ruth was already talking before she entered Taylor's office.

"Hello Ruth. How nice to see you," Taylor lied.

Ruth waved her pleasantry aside and sank with a whoosh in the proffered chair.

"I told Dominique not to go with a small press. Doubleday wanted her, but no, she had to sign with this 'we try harder—give more personal attention' poor excuse for a publishing company."

"Really Ruth, I don't think . . ."

"Apparently no one here does." Ruth's voice intensified.

Taylor leaned back in her chair and calmly placed her hands in her lap.

"What do you want Ruth?"

"What are you people going to do about Dominique's latest book?"

"Publish it," Taylor replied.

"I should think it would net you a tidy profit released posthumously."

"At this point we have two choices; release it after her death or not at all. It will do well. All her books sell well. It will make you the same revenue, Ruth, regardless. Does that answer your question?"

"The best interests of my client are my only concern. I wanted to be certain you," she struggled for the right word. "You publishers don't renege at your end, now that Dominique can't speak for herself."

"You came all the way from New York to tell me that? Couldn't you have called?" Taylor asked.

"No, of course not," Ruth said.

"I will attend the memorial service. Will there be a representative from Endicott, uh, Piñon Publishing?" She mispronounced piñon.

Taylor felt guilty. She didn't want to attend another funeral. Endicott's had been enough.

"I imagine several people will be there."

Ruth rose to leave, and flipped a long floral scarf over her shoulder.

"Ruth," Taylor stopped her. "Do you know if Dominique has any family?"

"No," she replied sharply. "No family." Ruth was gone in a blink.

Taylor wondered at Ruth's hostility. It was as if she were covering for something or someone, but why?

After a long day of editing Taylor walked out into the last few rays of sunshine rubbing her aching neck.

"Tough day?" Jim asked. He was casually sitting on the new company sign; his legs stretched out and crossed at the ankles.

"And then some. How about you?"

"Oh, the art work is about ready for Dominique's latest, and last, book." He grinned.

"Jim, why is all this so funny to you? People have died."

Taylor was irritated by the day's events.

"What else should I do? Can't bring'em back, might as well laugh. Preston was detestable. Dominique was, well, things will be a lot quieter without her."

"Since we're speaking so candidly Jim, Dominique was also quite good for business," Taylor said.

"Oh Taylor, my dear, lighten up. Life is short and all that."

Taylor was about to reply in kind when she spotted *the* car.

"Jim, is that Virginia's car?" She pointed at the large tan car parked across the street.

"No, hers is last year's model. Besides, she's not here. Remember? Are you still playing PI?"

"Very funny." Taylor crossed the pavement and looked inside the car for clues as to the owner. There was nothing lying on the seats or floor.

"Neat person."

She was about to walk on to her car when a movement near the office caught her eye.

"Jim, look over there. Did you see someone slide behind the chamisa?" She pointed to several large shrubs in yellow bloom.

"No, and you didn't either. Really Taylor, ever since your involvement with the good detective your imagination has gone viral."

"There is no *involvement* as you say," Taylor said defensively. "Once the investigation's over I'll probably never see him again."

"Me thinks the lady doth protest too much."

"Jim, shut up!" Taylor stormed off. He exasperated her at times. She turned quickly to retort.

"I know, I know," Jim mocked holding her back with his hands. "I'm being inappropriate again."

The look on Taylor's face set off a new round of mirth.

Taylor left without another thought to the person hiding in the bushes.

Chapter 18

T aylor had suffered from insomnia off and on since Dave's death. It was always different. Some nights she couldn't get to sleep; others she fell right to sleep only to awaken at two AM unable to go back to sleep. This was one of those nights. For the last hour she had taken deep breaths, progressively relaxed every part of her body, plumped the pillow and even resorted to counting sheep. She tossed back the comforter and buried a sleeping Oscar who quickly scrambled to follow her. It was time for her green tea and milk concoction. She wasn't sure it really worked or the boring habit of preparing it caused sleepiness.

She padded through the house in bare feet clad in her nightshirt; a navy cotton knit which hung to her knees. There was a nightlight in the kitchen so she saw no need to switch on any lights. She put on the kettle. To avoid making a mess, she poured milk by the light of the open refrigerator, and placed the small pan on a burner. Oscar materialized on the countertop. He was allowed to do this only for meals and night prowling. He sat regally awaiting his warm milk. Taylor poured some from the pan before it got too hot and set a saucer in front of him.

When the water was hot, she quickly steeped the green tea, added honey and topped it with the milk. A small squeeze of lemon finished her insomniac cocktail. Taylor pulled herself up on the counter next to Oscar. They sipped and lapped in happy companionship.

"Oscar, you love these nocturnal adventures, don't you? It's second nature to you feline types."

Oscar's only answer was to look up at her with his adorable clown markings and a spot of foamy white on his chin.

"Lick down Oscar." Taylor was about to demonstrate when she heard a loud explosion followed by glass shattering somewhere in the house.

Oscar practically dug under her to escape. She held him close and placed the other hand over her head should plaster begin dropping.

"Now what!" Fear cut through her body. It sounded more like a window rather than a vase or knickknack.

Her first instinct was to cower in the corner, but then Oscar regained his courage and was about to jump down from the counter to check it out.

"No Oscar."

She clasped his slender body with both hands and quietly slid down the lower cabinets to the floor. Holding the squirming cat with one hand, she opened the lower drawer. It was the deepest. She tossed the towels out, placed the cat inside and pushed his head down gently, closing the drawer.

"Please be quiet," she whispered.

Another piece of glass fell and splintered on her painstakingly refinished floor. Taylor wished there was a drawer big enough for her to crawl into. Instead she tried to become part of the kitchen.

Was someone in the house? She tried to listen, but her heart beat so loudly she was certain it would cover any sounds an intruder might make.

The landline hung on the wall opposite her in the breakfast nook. She had to do something and her cell was in the bedroom. She crawled along the floor edging slowing along the lower cabinets, in front of the stove, until the door to the dining room gaped uninvitingly. The distance across the opening was only a few feet, but it seemed huge to Taylor as she peered into the gloom. It looked empty, but she couldn't be sure no one was there.

She did what she later thought was a funny thing. She pulled her nightshirt down over her legs, so her skin wouldn't show, turned her back to the arched opening to conceal her face in the darkness with her hair, and crept by the doorway like a stealthy ninja. For a few moments she cringed against the wall.

With shaking hands she reached for the phone, pulled herself slowly upright and fumbled with the receiver. Her finger tried to punch in 9-1-1, but she missed the last digit. And then she remembered one-touch dialing! She depressed the button for emergencies.

The female voice who answered seemed so in control, but far away. Taylor gave her address first and then in a voice she was certain could not be heard she told the operator there might be someone in the house.

The operator relayed her message to dispatch and returned.

"Can you get out of the house?"

"I think so." Taylor looked across the room at the door to the garage. "Probably, but my cat?"

"Leave your cat. Get out of the house. The police are on the way."

Taylor held the receiver with a clenched hand, unwilling to give up the calm person on the other end. A person sitting in a room with other people; absolutely safe.

"Are you still there?" The voice asked. "Get out of the house. Now!"

She didn't want to, but the voice had been so certain. Taylor hung up and started for the door, fully upright this time and in a big hurry. The doorknob was within her grasp. Oscar scratched at the drawer. She knew when he realized his scratching was not being answered he would begin meowing loudly. She had to retrieve Oscar.

He had found his voice and was plaintively crying for release. Taylor tried to open the drawer without it squeaking and still grab Oscar before he ran off. She gave up, risked the noise and clutched the wiggling Aby. Oscar was tired of this game and hissed his discontent.

"Quiet Oscar. It's okay." Taylor tugged at the hand towel hanging from the stove and wrapped it around the angry cat.

Taylor wondered if her heart would survive its vigorous beating. Would it burst if the tension didn't break soon? Taylor raced across the kitchen to the door, but before she could open it a man appeared at the window. She shrank back out of sight holding Oscar in a death grip. He bit her thumb and she cried out, but managed to hold onto him.

"Police," a man called outside the door. She jumped.

"Anyone in there?" That was followed by a loud rap from a night stick.

Taylor regained some of her aplomb; hand poised to open the door, and then hesitated.

144

"Hold your badge up so I can see it through the peep hole." The officer complied.

"Vic, over here," he said while holding his badge.

Taylor opened the door.

"Why didn't you say so?"

She gave Detective Sanchez a withering look. Torn between the relief she felt that he was there, and her anger at him for somehow not knowing she needed help, gave her conflicting emotions. She sagged down cross-legged on the floor and cradled Oscar in her arms. A few tears escaped, but were quickly wiped away.

"Secure the structure," Victor said. Uniformed police swarmed throughout her house.

"Are you all right?" He squatted in front of her.

"What are you doing here? Do you live at that police station?"

Followed by: "I'm okay."

"Do you have a carrier?" he asked.

"Carrier?"

"For Oscar. I think he's had about enough. His eyes are bulging." He nodded toward the small cat with the large amber eyes.

Taylor relaxed her grip on Oscar and motioned to the pantry door.

"In there."

Victor placed the carrier next to Taylor and she gently pushed Oscar into the cage. He was happy to oblige.

"I'm going to set him in the pantry to keep him away from the noise." She left the door cracked so he could see her sitting at the table.

"Vic," one of the uniforms said. "Looks like someone shot once through the window in the master bedroom. Bullet's in the interior wall; glass all over the place."

145

"Any sign of the perp?"

"Negative. We're looking."

"Taylor," Victor said. "Do you have any idea who could have done this or why?"

"Of course not. All I know is, I moved here for the sunsets and tranquility." Taylor laughed moronically; hysteria about to overcome her.

"I'm going to make some more tea. I may sweeten it with Ativan. Do you want some?"

"No thanks but go ahead. Doing something will help you relax."

"That's why I'm doing it," she said testily.

Another uniformed officer brought her robe from the bedroom. She gratefully donned it and tied the belt.

"Did anything atypical happen today?" Victor asked. "Something that might explain this?"

"Atypical? Today? Why no, I'd say it's about the first day that nothing odd happened. Except . . ."

"What?" Victor prompted.

"Oh, it's probably nothing."

"Taylor, at this point everything is important."

"It's just I thought I saw someone hiding behind the bushes at the office."

"When?"

"This evening after work. Jim and I were looking at the car."

"What car?" Victor asked.

"The tan one. Like the one in the bookstore parking lot."

"You didn't mention seeing a tan car at the bookstore."

"Sure I did. You must have forgotten."

"Taylor, you've got to tell me these things. What year was the car?"

"It wasn't last year's model. Jim said so."

Victor spread his arms in an act of defeat.

"He says Virginia drives last year's model."

Taylor dropped a tea bag in a cup.

"Virginia? Virginia Compton? How is she connected?"

"I don't know she is, but someone driving a big tan car, possibly a Mercury, was leaving the bookstore parking lot when I drove in." She paused and filled her cup.

"Mercury doesn't make cars anymore," Victor said. "Could it have been another car?"

"It was American made," Taylor said. She tried to remember what the emblem looked like on the front of the car. "It was a Ford. I remember the circle with 'Ford' in it."

"Did I tell you the driver was wearing black? It couldn't be Virginia. She never wears black."

Victor wore a look of true affection and astonishment. Her mind worked in mysterious ways under pressure, not to mention how cute she looked in her rumpled robe.

"What are you staring at?" Taylor snapped as she stirred three teaspoons of sugar into her cup of tea.

"Do you know how much sugar you put in that?" he asked, grinning.

"I like it sweet." She drank every sickening drop of it.

Chapter 19

T he following morning Taylor witnessed the least funeral-ish service she had ever seen: Dominique Boucher's. There was no church service. Her wishes were to have the entire service done out of doors. It was to be a private affair. The office was closed, but Alise had volunteered to remain on phone duty. Everyone assembled at the mortuary where the cremation had been done. They piled into two limos wrapped in lavender bows. Ruth Standish, Virginia and Donald rode together. Taylor, Jim, Jessica and Candi filled the remaining car. Virginia was better off with Ruth than Jessica. The short procession headed north to the village of Tesuque.

"Why Tesuque?" Jim asked.

"Dominique owned some property and wanted her ashes scattered there," Jessica replied. "How's her book coming?" Jessica directed this question at Taylor.

"It's ready for line edit, but since Virginia's uh, no longer with us, I guess it'll have to go to a freelancer."

"Can't you do it?"

"I'm really not qualified to do it."

Jessica was beginning to annoy Taylor. They were on their way to a funeral and here she was talking shop.

"Virginia has years of experience. I don't. I think it should go to someone with more editing skills."

"Perhaps it's time you got the experience," Jessica snapped.

"Very well." Taylor did a quiet burn. It was Jessica's fault their best editor was now on permanent leave.

Less than thirty minutes later the cars moved through a crowd of perhaps fifty people dressed in various degrees of mourning attire. Some carried lighted candles. There were two security people keeping the milling group from the driveway. Flowers, many in lavender bows, dotted the ground next to the entrance. One of the guards opened the gate wrapped in a lavender ribbon.

"How did all these people find out where Dominique's service would be held?" Taylor asked.

"Twitter," Jim replied. "Ruth Standish Tweeted it yesterday.

"I'm not sure I follow her, but then I'd have to read my feed," Taylor added.

"My dear, you should follow everyone we work with," Jim said.

"Uh-huh." Social media was the last thing on her mind.

They drove through the gate onto a dirt road that curved through trees to a spacious clearing. A black van and a blue sedan were already parked.

"She must have planned to live here," Candi pointed to the slab that awaited a house.

"She certainly could afford it," added Jim. "I'd live here too if I could; one of the best addresses in the area."

"If you don't count Wilderness Gate," Candi observed.

The black van looked ominous until three men

dressed in kilts and holding bagpipes emerged.

"Bagpipes?" Taylor raised an eyebrow.

"Ruth Standish made the arrangements. I assume she's carrying out Dominique's wishes," Jim said.

"Funny, she was in my office yesterday and didn't say a thing about making arrangements," Taylor said. "I thought she came all the way from New York to lambast Piñon Publishing and our haphazard handling of Dominique's royalty statements.

"What can I say; she's as peculiar as Dominique. Maybe they were friends," Jim surmised.

The group gathered on the far side of the concrete slab and stood silently waiting for whatever was about to occur. It was a cloudy day, but not raining as it had at Preston's service. From within the trees bagpipes played *Amazing Grace*. The eerily beautiful music drifted across the clearing wavering in intensity as the musicians approached the small gathering.

When the last note had played, the minister, obviously a member of an alternative sect, read Dylan Thomas' poem *Do Not Go Gentle Into That Good Night*. There was no eulogy and no need for one. Everyone was aware of Dominique's many accomplishments. The ashes were shaken from a lavender urn among the tall ponderosa pine and golden aspen as the young bearded minister swung a censer of burning incense. Its fragrance mingled with the pine. A mourning dove called nearby.

One woman in a black veil stood alone. Taylor wondered who she was; a fan, long-lost family or friend?

Taylor could well imagine Dominique raging against the dying of the light. She mourned her loss to the literary world. Dominique had been a fine writer and a brilliant storyteller. She would miss her for those reasons.

* * *

After the service, they returned to the office. Alise was grateful to see them. Mission Control had proved more difficult to man than she expected.

"I don't know how Candi does it," Alise said. "This has everything but the nuclear codes!"

A small white handkerchief tied to a pencil edged its way through Taylor's office door.

"Okay if I come in?" teased Jim.

One boot toe tested his welcome.

"Come in Jim," Taylor said. "After the night I had and the funeral this morning, I can stand even you."

"Gee thanks Taylor. I don't know when I've been more touched."

"Sorry."

"That's okay." He seated himself comfortably. "So what happened last night?"

Taylor told him the whole scary incident, careful to leave out her nearly incoherent remarks made to Detective Sanchez.

"You shoved Oscar into a drawer? I bet he liked that!"

"Not really, but I had to do something with him."

"Sounds like you did fine. Did the good detective think it had anything to do with the murders?"

"I'm sure he does. What I can't figure out is what I could possibly know that would threaten the killer?"

"You've read the manuscript," Jim pointed out.

"While it is similar to our mystery, it certainly did not point any fingers. The murderer in the book was the mistress. Does that apply in this case?"

"Hmm," Jim rubbed his chin. "What about Virginia?"

Taylor was surprised Jim would think of Virginia in that way.

"I thought of her, but Jim, do you really think she is capable of murder? And, was she Preston's mistress? I don't want to believe that."

"First," Jim said. "Every one of us is capable of killing. Whether we actually do the deed depends on the circumstances and what motivates us. I'm including self-defense in my observation."

"In that case, I guess I could agree, but what about Virginia? Could she have been Preston's lover?"

"Donald says he referred to her as the love of his life in his will."

"So I heard."

"Donald was plenty steamed about it. Endicott left $500,000 to Virginia and only $5,000 to him."

"Since when did he start talking? I thought he was holed up in his office counting his fingers."

"Since the reading of the will, but it's not like a conversation, more like mumbling as he punches numbers into his computer."

"Why would he leave any money at all to Donald? He's a good accountant from what I know, but that's all."

"Maybe because he is a lowly accountant. Gee Taylor, how would I know? I hadn't given it much thought. All I know is Donald is livid, for him at least, about the whole thing."

Taylor thought back to the day she visited Donald's mother. The faded splendor of their home was testimony to a limited income; an income used primarily to pay for medical treatment. Unless they were hiding money in a mattress, Taylor couldn't imagine there was any excess.

"Hey Taylor." Jim snapped his fingers. "Anyone home?"

"Oh, sorry. I was thinking."

"How about you stop thinking and let's take the after-noon off. The aspens are at peak color. We can drive up to the ski basin and take the lift to the summit. Do you a world of good."

"Oh Jim. I can't take off. Look at this mess. With Virginia gone I just couldn't."

"Best time to do it, when you need it the most. Besides, you never take off."

He leaned over her desk and tousled her hair.

"Come on," he teased. "Just say yes."

"Oh, okay!" She gave in. "Let's do it." Jim could be so charming when he tried.

"Good. Meet you in the parking lot."

By one-thirty they were driving Hyde Park Road in Jim's Jeep. Although the road steadily climbed it didn't have many switchbacks for the first half of the drive. After that, it was one sharp turn after another. Jim steadfastly refused to follow the speed limits and Taylor found herself getting a bit dizzy as he took the corners too fast.

"Jim, would you please back off a little. This is supposed to be a relaxing drive."

"Sure. But those speed limits are for the snow season."

"Right." Taylor didn't believe it for a moment but she didn't want to argue with Jim. It was too easy. She decided to concentrate on the spectacular stands of autumn aspen quivering in the light breeze. Every turn up the mountain brought more glorious color, sometimes mixed with the deep green of the pines. On the shady side of the mountain colors were intense. On the bright side, the light played through the trees diffusing the color into a vast yellow glow.

They made it to the top in good time, given Jim's

demonstrated defiance of lawful limits. Since it was a weekday there were few leaf peepers. On weekends it could be a very slow trip indeed. She remembered following a lumbering old Cadillac on another fall day. It had taken her and Dave nearly an hour to climb Mount Baldy. But it had been worth it.

"Here we are." Jim pulled the Jeep into a parking space at the Santa Fe ski area. "Last one to the top buys lunch."

Lunch? Taylor didn't recall lunch being mentioned before now. She let it go; more than enough time later to squirm out of that.

Jim bought their tickets and they waited in a short line for the Super Chief.

"Ski much?" he asked.

"Rank beginner. At this point my best record is down the bunny slope with only one mishap. About half the time I can't get off the lift without falling."

"You'll have to buy a season ticket and practice. I'd be glad to come with you; give you pointers if you want."

"Uh-huh."

"We're next," Jim nudged her elbow.

They sat back in the four-seater as it swung up in a smooth motion. It brought to mind Taylor's first experience on a lift. She had been absolutely terrified. It seemed to move so fast and at each pole it bumped twice. She was certain archaeologists would someday discover the impressions left on the lift bar by her white-knuckled fingers.

The sun was high in the sky. Gone were the clouds of Dominique's service. For a few moments the lift stopped to allow someone time to be seated. The absolute quiet was heavenly. Jim seemed to appreciate it too, since he made no attempt at conversation. Taylor closed her eyes and felt the sun on her face. Last night's events took their place on a back burner while she enjoyed the trip to the top.

The lift began moving again and they exclaimed at the beauty of the glowing aspen and evergreen forest. At the top they got off the lift at the platform and walked across the summit to look at Santa Fe below.

Taylor thought she could see forever from this spot on the mountain. The Jemez range to the west was a distant blue. The elevation was 11,250 feet according to the sign erected by the Santa Fe National Forest. Taylor could barely see the Pedernal Georgia O'Keeffe had repeatedly painted from her Ghost Ranch home. After her death, her ashes were scattered at the top of Pedernal.

"Aren't you glad you live here?" Jim asked.

"Oh yes. I can't imagine living anywhere else now. Santa Fe has everything."

"Don't forget the inflated cost of living due to the tourism industry. And the limited water supply," Jim added.

Taylor frowned at him.

"Jim, has anyone ever told you your outlook is a bit on the pessimistic side?"

"You, my lovely." He grinned wickedly and cupped her chin.

"I prefer to think of it as pragmatic."

"Whatever. But it can be a bit of a drag."

"I resolve to not be a drag." He punched her shoulder playfully.

"Let's go eat. I'm starving."

Lunch consisted of hot dogs and fries eaten on the sun deck. Red picnic tables with umbrellas, provided respite from the rigors of skiing, and now offered a quiet place under the turquoise sky.

"Browning," Jim said, gulping soda. "Tell me about yourself."

"I'm an open book. What you see is what you get."

"No, tell me about your life before your gig being our editor extraordinaire."

"Born and raised in St. Louis, married Dave and moved to Denver for his job. Now I'm in Santa Fe."

"That was fast," Jim said. "I nearly got whiplash."

She laughed and it was spontaneous rather than forced. She was having fun and it felt good. Maybe Jim was right, you might as well laugh. Oh good heavens, what a thought; Jim right?

* * *

By the time they returned to the office it was after five.

"Surely, you're not going in," Jim said. "After I rescued you from it all."

"Just to pick up a manuscript; I can do some reading tonight."

"Not me. I'll see you Monday." He gunned the Jeep's motor and was off.

Taylor used her new key card and walked in the quiet office. She chose the manuscript she wanted to read. Three steps from the lobby, she heard noises from the basement. She inhaled sharply and stopped.

Curious, she headed downstairs.

She turned at the landing and stood for a moment looking down the hall. The only light was coming from Donald's office. She'd take a quick look and see what he was up to.

At the base of the stairs she stepped on a crumbled piece of paper. The office below became silent.

"Who's there? Jim?" called Donald.

"It's me, Taylor."

"What are you doing here?" She heard a drawer close with a thud.

"Picking up a manuscript."

He came into view as she stepped into the hall.

"I heard noise and wanted to see who was down here. How are you?"

"Fine," he said tersely. "Just trying to finish a few things before sales conference."

"Sales conference isn't until December," Taylor said. "Why the hurry?"

"Then it will be end-of-the-year reports." he said defensively.

Donald did not want her down here. The ball of paper had given away her descent. He'd had time to hide whatever he was really working on. She was beginning to suspect nearly everyone of something.

"Well, I must get home to Mother." He crammed some papers into his briefcase. "She worries if I'm late." He moved to leave.

"Aren't you coming?" It was more of a statement than a question. Taylor acquiesced and joined Donald on the steps. When they locked up Taylor waited for Donald to walk with her to the parking lot. Instead he said goodnight and walked off in the other direction.

"Isn't your car in the lot?" Taylor asked Donald's retreating back.

"Nope. Parked in the street."

157

Taylor couldn't remember ever seeing Donald in his car. Now that she wanted to know what kind of vehicle he drove, he wasn't cooperating.

In the parking lot she found her Mustang and a tan Crown Vic. Maybe a visitor was taking a chance on parking there. Taylor made a mad dash for her Pony. She was feeling spooked.

Chapter 20

Monday morning Taylor couldn't see the top of her desk. Most of Virginia's work had already made its way to her office.

"This is ridiculous." She made the short trip to Jessica's office.

"She's not here." Alise frowned.

"Will she be in soon?"

"I don't know. She wasn't in yesterday afternoon either."

"Can she be reached?" Taylor was exasperated. She hadn't known Jessica long enough to know if she would be a dependable, responsible employer. This was not a normal situation. Concern wedged its way into her thoughts.

"I haven't had any luck reaching her," Alise said. "All I get is her voice mail, and I've left several messages. She didn't even tell me she was leaving."

Alise was vexed. How could she do her job when her boss never told her where she was going or how to reach her.

"What's her address?" Taylor was concerned.

159

"Go ahead," Alise said. "I'll text it to you."

Taylor left Alise to pull up her address book. By the time she reached the parking lot, the address showed up on her phone. It was in the city's east side. Jessica's house was one street east of Canyon Road, the art center of Santa Fe.

A few minutes later she turned onto Alameda. The Santa Fe River was on her right as she drove east. It became a river only during spring snow melt or after a heavy downpour; most of the time it was more of a trickle. Nonetheless, it was a very pleasant place to walk. Picnic tables were scattered along the edge of the river and a number of people were taking advantage of the lovely morning by strolling aimlessly. One serious jogger zipped by the walkers. Taylor wished she had time for a walk but Jessica's absence caused her concern.

She wanted to talk with Jessica about the possibility of bringing Virginia back to work if only until a replacement could be found. Taylor hoped to persuade her to see Virginia's importance and commitment to the publishing company, but Alise's comments about not being able to locate her had struck an alarming chord.

She reached the right block and slowed to watch for Jessica's house number. On the right among the tall trees was the house, and what a house. Taylor drove across a small wooden bridge just wide enough for one car to squeeze across to a parking area beneath the trees. The Mustang's tires crunched and sank a bit in the soft gravel. The adobe structure was two-storied with a three-car garage. One garage door was open revealing Jessica's black Mercedes sport car inside. Her car accounted for, was Jessica at home or merely left her garage door open?

Taylor walked along a flagstone path sheltered by a trellis. In spring wisteria would be in bloom, with delicate, fragrant flower clusters hanging like grapes from the vine. At the door she paused, aware of how quiet it was. A feeling of isolation crept over her as she considered what to do. She rang the doorbell and waited. Several moments passed. No one answered.

Her anxiety was increasing. She looked through the sidelight next to the front door. Although there was a white panel curtain, she could still see the sunlit foyer. Tile covered the floor where a grandfather clock ticked contentedly. There was a nicho full of tiny folk art pieces. Everything seemed right with the world.

She moved around the corner of the house until she reached a window she could see through. Here, she could hear a blaring noise, but couldn't identify it. This was the kitchen. What she saw nearly made her heart stop.

There were two pots on the stove, acrid smoke rising from both of them. It was the fire alarm she heard. If someone was in the house they couldn't help but hear the piercing sound. The room was a hazy mess. If someone didn't turn off the burners, there would be a fire soon. Was Jessica in the house, but unable to call for help?

Taylor dug for her phone. But who should she call? There was no fire yet. She didn't know if an ambulance was needed. Maybe the police? She'd try to get in first and turn off the stove.

River rocks had been used as landscaping around the back of the house. Taylor picked one about the size of a brick and ran into the garage. If only the connecting door to the house had a window. It didn't.

"Blast!" Taylor raced back to the rear courtyard. The kitchen had a large eating area next to the house which opened onto a terrace. Before crashing one of the panes in the French doors, she looked through the door at the lock.

"Double cylinder! I'll never break that down."

The kitchen window was her best chance. She stepped back and lobbed the stone at the window. The pane broke, but there was a stubborn screen causing the stone to bounce back and fall to the ground.

At that moment the security alarm sounded. Help would be on the way soon. She thought it odd that the smoke alarm wasn't connected to the home security. Taylor pounded the screen with the stone until it tore and she could pull it back, then she broke the remaining glass so she could crawl through without getting cut.

The scorching smell was overwhelming as Taylor fell through the now open window onto a bench below. She double-timed it across the expansive kitchen, vaulted the bar, and switched off both burners. Taylor nearly burned her fingers turning off the controls. An oven mitt lay on the counter. She slipped it on taking extreme care to move the hot pans to the sink, a column of smoke flowed from each. The food had burned to a black crusty mess and the burners still glowed. The pots screamed in agony as the hot surfaces met with the cool stainless steel of the sink.

Taylor raced through the house checking each room for Jessica. Any other time, she would have enjoyed exploring this house. Meticulous care had been taken in both the design and construction. A glance into the elegant dining room showed only a very expensive Taos original table and hutch, an antique chandelier and hammered tin mirror.

She crossed the foyer to the other side of the house and found the living room filled with wooden furniture covered in overstuffed ivory cushions. White walls had a life of their own as the giant fireplace bounced yellow light from faux logs set in teepee style. Peach accent pillows spilled off the sofa onto the floor by design. The room would have been warm and inviting any other time. Even Jessica's study was in perfect order, just like her office at work.

A quick look at the guest wing revealed nothing more than two lovely bedrooms with en suite baths beautifully furnished in southwest style. Fresh flowers were placed in each room and bookshelves bulged with books and folk art for her guests. That left only the upstairs. The curving staircase seemed somehow menacing.

Taylor took the staircase by twos. The piercing alarm was even louder upstairs and she prayed for the sound of a siren soon. Just how long did it take for the police to arrive? If the worst had happened, she would rather someone else found Jessica.

A four-poster bed dominated the master suite. Burgundy awning striped chairs, placed thoughtfully near a window made it possible to read or watch the mountains at sunset. Flowers were placed on every available flat surface. Taylor would love to have her flower budget to live on; it would likely exceed her salary.

The only place Taylor hadn't looked was the master bath. With the alarm still screeching she had no way to know if someone was in the house. There would be no tell-tale squeaking floor boards to warn her.

She reached the entrance to the bath and cautiously looked around. No one! What she saw next made her want to turn tail. The curved shower wall was built-in. A wall of peach tile and glass brick made a luxurious shower. Only one problem; in order to reach the shower Taylor had to walk into and around the wall of tile. She inched her way down the incline and wished she had armed herself with something, anything. There was plenty of light thanks to a skylight. Taylor braced herself as she took one last step into the abyss. Empty!

"I'm going to be arrested for breaking and entering." Taylor let out all the air from her lungs at once. She hadn't dared to breathe as she entered the shower.

"Furthermore, I'll be the latest suspect in two murders. After all, if one kills people, burglary is no big deal." Her relief at not finding Jessica was quickly pushed away as she pondered her fate.

Downstairs she waited in the foyer for the police to arrive. The search of the house had only taken a few minutes, but it had seemed an eternity. She was about to go outside to get away from the noise when she noticed a door she hadn't seen before. It was off the entrance hall. When she looked down at the floor, there was water spreading beneath the door and into the foyer.

With pounding heart, Taylor opened the door. Jessica was lying on the powder room floor. The rug was soaked with water. The faucet was running and the sink was overflowing. Jessica appeared to be asleep except for the cut on her forehead which oozed a little blood. She had apparently fallen and hit her head. Taylor hoped for the best.

Jessica had a faint pulse in her neck. Taylor wanted to make her more comfortable, but was afraid to move her. She turned off the running water in the sink and sent the remainder down the drain.

Two officers burst into the foyer, guns drawn but pointed downward.

"No need for guns," Taylor squeaked. "Get an ambulance." She slowly stood when commanded to only to sink as her knees crumpled beneath her. Everything went blessedly black.

When she woke a few minutes later, the alarm was still blasting. No, it was a different sound, and she was moving.

"You're fine," the EMT told her patting her arm. "I'm

Adam. We're taking you to hospital to be checked out. Just relax."

"Relax! Was I shot? Am I hurt?"

The whole terrifying kerfuffle came back to her. Was she shot? Had the officer thought her a murderer and shot her? Taylor concentrated on her body. There was no pain.

"You're fine. No bullet wounds. You just fainted." Adam assured her.

"How's Jessica?" she asked.

"She's in the ambulance ahead of us. Don't worry. She'll get the best help."

The way he said it she believed him where her condition was concerned, but she wasn't so sure about Jessica.

Chapter 21

When Taylor awoke the first thing she saw was a nurse adjusting the covers on her bed. She was a large woman in green scrubs. Her grey hair was short and in soft curls against her head.

"Hello Hon. How are you feeling?"

"Sleepy," Taylor's tongue felt thick and heavy. In fact, all of her body felt heavy. "What happened to me?"

"The doctor gave you a sedative. We gather you had quite an adventure today." The nurse smiled reassurance and patted her hand. She had kind blue eyes. In her fuzzy state Taylor focused on those eyes.

"What time is it?"

"Nearly six in the evening."

"I have to get home and feed my cat."

"Now Hon, you just stay put. The doctor's keeping you in overnight." Her gentle hands pushed Taylor back against the pillow.

Taylor groaned.

"Say, there is someone here to see you. He made me promise to tell him soon as you were awake." She left before

Taylor could ask who.

"She's worried about her cat." The nurse said to someone in the hall.

"Here's your visitor."

Detective Sanchez knocked hesitantly on the door. "Mind if I come in?"

Taylor tried to wave her hand, but it seemed like too much trouble to lift it. Both arms felt like lumps.

"Please do." Her voice steadied.

"You're worried about Oscar? You must be okay. If you want, I'll go by and feed him. I don't think they're letting you out tonight."

"Thank you. I would appreciate that. I hate to look a gift horse in the mouth, but Oscar has his own way of getting fed." Taylor described how he must leave the cabinet door open so Oscar could go inside and turn around, and then jump up on the counter. "It's okay he's on the counter. He knows what area he's allowed."

"Oo-kay," Victor said cautiously. "I'm not going to need my cuffs, am I?"

"I don't think Oscar would stand still long enough for you to cuff him." She smiled at the image.

"I'm told my purse is in that drawer. The keys are in the outside pocket."

"Got them."

"Why do I have to stay overnight? I feel fine."

"You look a bit woozy to me," Victor said. "You don't do many drugs, do you?"

There were times when Victor's sense of humor was rather irritating to Taylor. This was one of them. It suddenly came to her why she was in the hospital.

"Oh, dear God. Jessica? Is she alright?"

"She has stabilized." He grinned. "I believe that is

167

doctor-ese for it. They are running tests. We should know soon what's wrong with her."

"Poison?"

"Not sure yet. Regardless, she has a much better chance here in the hospital. If you hadn't found her the outcome could have been far worse."

Taylor sighed. "Then it was worth it."

"What? Oh, you mean the B and E, as we call it in our vernacular." Victor teased.

Taylor tried to glare at him, but her eyes wouldn't quite focus. She settled for a frown.

"I had a feeling about her."

"Are we talking about women's intuition? You know, I don't believe that is based in scientific fact."

Now she was aggravated. So much so she was caught completely off guard when he learned over and kissed her lightly on the forehead. In fact, she was speechless.

"Next time you get one of those feelings," Victor admonished softly. "Would you please call me first? I've grown rather attached to you and would like to see you live out a full life." He left Taylor astonished and emotional. She hated that.

* * *

The following morning Taylor padded down the corridor in the ugly scuffs provided by the hospital. She had covered her hospital gown in a sheet from the bed. It was better than trying to be ladylike in the open back. The hospital would release her before lunch, and she wanted to check on Jessica before she left.

Jessica's room was the last on the right. Taylor knocked softly on the half open door.

"Jessica, are you up to some company?"

"Come in Taylor."

Light from the window washed the color from Jessica's face accentuating the brassiness of her hair. She was sitting up and appeared much improved from yesterday when Taylor found her on the floor.

"You look a lot better conscious. How do you feel?" Taylor asked.

"Embarrassed."

"Why?" Taylor asked in surprise. "What on earth do you have to be embarrassed about?"

"Taylor," she motioned to the chair. "Please sit down. You've been through quite an ordeal yourself."

Once Taylor settled herself in the uncomfortable chair, with her cold feet tucked beneath her, Jessica continued.

"It seems I have the flu. The tests didn't show any evidence of poisoning."

"But that's great, not that you have the flu, but no attempt was made on your life. That's good news. If anyone should be embarrassed, it's me. I'm the one who made like the cavalry."

"No, not at all. My doctor said you may well have saved my life. Flu can be a serious illness, and add a concussion to that, the potential is deadly."

"How did you fall?"

"I was preparing a late lunch when the food odors began making me nauseous. I went in the bathroom to splash my face with water. When I leaned over the sink, the room started to spin. That's the last thing I remember before waking here in the hospital. If I hadn't died from the flu, or the fall, it's possible I would have died in the fire."

"Fire?"

"The food on the stove. I would have sworn I turned off the burners. Eventually, there would have been a fire." Jessica leaned toward Taylor. "I'm convinced you saved my life. Thank you."

Taylor was touched by Jessica's sincerity. She stood and clasped Jessica's hand.

"I'm glad I overreacted."

"If there's anything I can do for you please ask."

Taylor considered for a moment whether to reply. She knew exactly what she wanted to ask Jessica, but wasn't sure this was the time. She decided to go for it.

"There is something you could do for the company," Taylor said. "Would you consider bringing back Virginia?"

Jessica's face took on a hard edge. Taylor was afraid she had gone too far.

"She is a good editor. Even Dominique liked her. Just think about it?"

"Okay, I'll think it over."

"Well, I'm about to be sprung. I should go get dressed and you need the rest."

"Thanks again, Taylor."

Taylor smiled and nodded. She didn't trust her voice. There was something profound about saving someone's life. She would never forget that day. Taylor had been so self-involved after Dave's death it felt good to find she was able to put aside her own concerns. She felt as if she'd turned a big corner in her recovery.

Chapter 22

"Your carriage awaits." Jim opened the door of his Jeep and extended his hand to Taylor.

"I don't understand why I have to be wheeled out of the hospital," Taylor said with rancor.

Jim grinned at the long-suffering orderly.

"She gets testy every time we have to hospitalize her."

The young man nodded politely. He was accustomed to complaining patients. They all thought they could walk out of the hospital. They probably could, but not as long as he was in charge. Rules were rules.

When Taylor was seated and belted in—Jim insisted on doing this for her—he winked at the orderly who gave him the thumbs up sign.

"Off we go," Jim said.

The engine protested a bit; then started.

"Needs a tune-up," Jim said apologetically.

"I hear our favorite detective fed one furious cat last night. I would have been happy to take care of the little guy. Sanchez dropped off your house keys. Here they are."

He tossed them to Taylor who let her lap catch them.

This was just what Taylor needed, two grown men fighting over who fed Oscar while she spent a night in hospital.

"He was there and offered, so I gave him my keys with my thanks."

"If I'd known you were in the hospital, I would have been there too."

"I'm sorry, but for awhile I was unconscious and unable to think about calling anyone."

"No need to fret," Jim said condescendingly and patted her knee.

Taylor wanted to kill him but there had been enough murders in Santa Fe lately. Instead of encouraging him along this line of conversation she watched the piñon and chamisa go by in a blur as Jim sped north on Old Pecos Trail.

"Here we are."

Jim set the Jeep's brake and ran around to help her out. Taylor had enough of all this help and got out before Jim could reach her. To her surprise she felt a bit dizzy.

"Hey, hey," Jim said with concern and placed his arm firmly around her waist.

"You've been through quite an ordeal. Don't try to be a hero. You did that yesterday."

Oscar was not overjoyed to see her. After all, she had abandoned him with no warning whatever. He allowed her to pick him up, but turned his head to avoid any eye contact.

"You're in deep doo-doo now," Jim observed.

"Oh, he'll get over it, but it may take a few days. He thinks I deserted him."

"He *thinks*!" Jim scoffed. "Taylor, my love, this whole

situation is affecting your otherwise razor sharp mind. I want you to lie down the rest of the day. Direct order from Dr. Jim. Need any help?"

"Out!" Taylor pointed to the door. "Out!"

"Okay, okay, I'm going." The last thing Taylor heard was Jim on her front portal mocking her. "Oscar thinks; the cat thinks. It's a miracle!"

* * *

A few days later Jessica had recovered and was back at work. Taylor had beaten her back to work by two days. Things had been pretty quiet, just like before the murders, except for a mammoth pile of manuscripts that increased in height every day. Taylor started stacking them in a corner of her office so she wouldn't have to look at them.

"Taylor." Jessica stood in her door. "I thought about what you said at the hospital. Virginia will be returning this morning. You were right about her being good for the company. And obviously, you are inundated with so much work there is no way you can do it all."

"Thank you Jessica." Taylor felt relief and hoped the two women could coexist.

"How are you feeling?" Taylor thought this would be a safe subject.

"Good, a bit weak, but that's to be expected. I'm glad to be back at work."

After Jessica left, Taylor pushed a stack of manuscripts aside and placed an upcoming mystery in the middle of her desk. The type was set and it was ready to become an ARC from which advance reviews could be done.

Galleys needed to be ordered. She hurriedly chose a

cover stock color, requested a smaller size to keep the cost down, and placed a photocopy of the book cover on top of the stack. After scrawling some instructions to the galley printer she tried to assemble a box to ship it in. There simply wasn't space on her desk.

Now that Virginia was returning, there was no point in keeping all these manuscripts. She heaved the stack with a groan and carried it into Virginia's office placing it on her credenza. When she turned to leave she couldn't help noticing Virginia's computer was on.

The same sentence repeated until it filled the screen. Curiosity overwhelmed Taylor and she sat down in the chair for a closer look.

A scream rose in her throat that she was able to suppress, covering her mouth with her hand. The entire screen was comprised of one sentence, "She must die."

She hurriedly swung around in the chair to see if anyone was there; no one. The fine hairs on her neck prickled. She herself had asked Jessica to bring Virginia back into the fold. Could she have been wrong about Virginia? And was this a threat against Virginia or another woman at the company?

Taylor rushed to Jessica's office. Empty. Alise was gone from her desk. She was never around when needed. She called Candi from Jessica's office.

"Candi, do you know where Jessica is?" She tried to steady her voice.

"Sure," Candi said. "She left with Virginia a while ago in Virginia's new car."

"Where'd they go?"

"Said they were going to work out something. Jessica left orders to take messages. They will be gone for an hour or so."

"You said Virginia has a new car? What does it look like?"

"Like the other one only new. I can't tell any difference."

"Thanks," Taylor mumbled. Her fingers fumbled as she tried to dial the phone.

"Detective Sanchez is out of the office right now," the desk attendant said. "Want to leave a message?" *He insists I call him when something happens and then he's not there.*

She left her name and number with the operator and promptly left the office.

Since they had gone by car that left out a number of places within walking distance. But where did they go? There were hundreds of restaurants in Santa Fe, more than most cities its size. It was also possible they did not go to a restaurant but it did seem the mostly likely place. Virginia did not like hot, spicy foods but they were unlikely to eat a meal. Drinks were more likely.

Taylor paused before she started her car. If Virginia intended to kill Jessica she wouldn't take her to a restaurant to do it. Or would she? If Jessica was the killer, would she try to slip poison in Virginia's drink?

With the awareness she simply could not find them in time to save a life, she drove to the police station.

* * *

Victor Sanchez strode into the lobby where Taylor had been waiting.

"Why do you leave me a message and then take off to places unknown?" he said.

175

"We don't have time for this prattle. Virginia and Jessica are somewhere in the city together, in Virginia's car."

"I don't follow?"

"Virginia's car is a tan Crown Vic, just like her old one. You remember? Like the one at the bookstore."

"Okay, so what are you saying?"

"I went into Virginia's office to leave some queries. They were piled sky-high, and since Jessica told me Virginia was returning I wanted them out of my office."

"Go on."

"That's when I saw it on the computer screen."

"What?"

"A sentence was typed over and over. It said 'She must die.'"

"Stay here," Victor dashed off to alert dispatch.

Taylor's knees felt a bit shaky. She wanted to sit but couldn't help but wonder who had already sat there. Santa Fe wasn't a crime-ridden place, but it had its share of unsavory characters. All of whom had probably sat in this very room in these chairs.

"Okay," Victor said behind her. She jumped. That amused him.

"We're looking for them. Now go back to work and don't worry."

"Don't worry? Are you kidding? Do you realize I asked Jessica to bring her back? If she kills Jessica, it will be my fault."

"I admit this looks bad, but there's nothing more you can do so get on with your day. If I hear any news, I'll give you a call."

Taylor swung by the office and let herself in. It was getting late and the place was deserted. She was drawn back to Virginia's office. She found Virginia's computer shut

176

down, the screen black. For a moment she thought maybe she had imagined the awful words on its screen.

At her own desk she straightened the mess she'd left. Someone had turned off her computer too. But who? A conscientious employee or the killer?

Taylor almost missed seeing the CD on the credenza. If she hadn't made the effort to bring order to her office, she would have overlooked it.

She turned on her computer, inserted the CD and waited for the directory. There was only one document saved, "For You."

The retrieved file made Taylor go cold. She felt her chest constrict and found it difficult to breathe. It was similar to Virginia's screen earlier only the text read over and over, "You're next!" She scrolled down the page only to find more of the same.

The walls seemed to press in against her. She felt entombed. And she was no longer alone.

Someone was coming upstairs. She was sure she heard footsteps. She ejected the CD and hid it in the middle drawer of her desk, picked up a message slip and pretended to read it.

"Working hard Taylor?" Thank heavens it was Donald. Taylor looked up and tried to appear normal.

"Still working." She smiled.

"Made some tea," he said. "Care to have one? I have more downstairs." He placed the steaming cup on her blotter.

"Thanks," she mumbled. She didn't want tea or talk. All she wanted was to get out!

"You okay?" Donald asked.

"Yes. Thanks. I'm in a bit of a hurry is all. Virginia's back, but we're struggling to catch up with the editing chores."

"I'll leave you to it."

With Donald gone, Taylor poured the tea in the flower pot containing her only plant, a poorly palm that probably didn't have a chance of survival with her as its caretaker. Her memory always failed her when it came to caring for them. Only when she noticed them gasping their last would she think to water them. It would appreciate the drink.

She cupped her head with her hands and tried to think. But she couldn't think here. Not where so many things had happened. Victor was right; she should have stayed out of this. It was all so unreal. She was afraid, afraid she was going to be the next victim.

Chapter 23

After finding the CD, Taylor delivered it to Victor on her way home. Once he saw the contents he insisted Taylor not go anywhere, except work or home, until the case was solved. When she insisted eating was a necessity, he instructed her to take Jim along.

"I don't like him much, but we no longer feel he's a suspect."

A real vote of confidence.; Jim had been happy to escort her. Too happy.

"Hey Taylor," Jim said over the intercom the following afternoon. "I'm going to take a cab to the garage and pick up my car. Its tune-up is a *fait accompli*. You ready to call it a day?"

"I really need to finish proofing this cover blueline. It needs to go back to the printer by overnight mail. Why don't you go ahead? I should have it done by the time you get back."

"That's not following the detective's orders."

"Oh, give me a break. I don't have to be watched every second."

179

"Are you the only one left up there?"

"Just me." She touched her plant. It didn't look too good. No surprise.

"I guess it will be all right. I'll lock you in. By the way, there's a storm brewing over the mountains. I'll try to get back and pick you up before it hits. See you later."

She looked closely at every word and image. Bluelines resemble blue prints in color and the type of paper. Since they are made from the final film and are used to make the plates that print the book, it is important they are accurate. It is expensive to make corrections at this stage of publication so only actual errors will be noted, no rewriting at this phase.

Taylor had been both relieved and discomfited when Virginia and Jessica returned to the office after their meeting yesterday; both in good health.

"Oh no!" She found an error that had to be corrected. Taylor searched her desk for the small orange sticky notes they used to mark mistakes and came up empty-handed. That meant a trip to the supply room in the basement.

Thunder rumbled in the distance. A shudder ran down her back as she flipped on the light to the basement stairs. The supply room was the last room downstairs. She passed Jim's office and then Donald's. His door was closed, but there was a light on. Not the overhead, but perhaps a lamp. He must be gone, there wasn't a sound. Not even a clicking keyboard.

The room was well stocked: paper, art supplies, book catalogs, art work, ads and promotional materials were everywhere. The office supplies were on the right, behind the door. Jim's painted-spattered overalls hung on the back of the door. The package of sticky notes was on a shelf near the floor. Taylor pulled one pant leg out of the way so she could reach an orange pad.

Odd thing, there was a brown paint smear on one leg. It was different from the other paint stains which were actually small flecks of color. The legs were clean except for this one long smudge. The color seemed familiar. It was the color of the building. Someone had gotten too close to the wet paint. How did they get it on the inside of the leg? If one had bumped against the wall the stain would have been on the outside of the trousers.

"Looking for something?"

Taylor nearly hit her head on a shelf when she jumped. Donald was standing in the doorway.

"You scared me half to death," Taylor said and covered her chest with her hand to steady an out of control heart.

"Oh sorry." It didn't seem sincere. She thought for a moment he had actually tried to scare her.

"I've got some reports to work on, tax season is coming," he said. "Would you care for a drink? Tea, coffee, soft drink? Our fridge is well-stocked. I was about to put on the kettle for tea myself."

"Thank you, but I don't care for anything right now. I came down for some sticky notes and now that I've got them I'll go back to my office. I've got a blueline that needs to go out tonight."

"You looked very interested in the overalls. Why?"

There was something about Donald that made her uncomfortable. Taylor thought perhaps all accountants were that way. A world full of numbers didn't hold many people. Maybe he had trouble socializing and chose a profession that kept him away from other people. She decided to keep the paint on the overalls to herself until she could figure out why it bothered her.

"No. They were just in my way," she said. "This

room's so crowded; it's hard to find what I need." She made to leave, but he seemed to be blocking her exit.

"Excuse me, Donald, but I do need to get back to work."

"I really must insist that you have that drink with me." His tone of voice had changed and it was harsh.

"Insist? I don't understand."

"Is it clear now?" Donald pulled a small gun from his jacket pocket.

"Donald, for heaven's sake, is that a gun? Are you trying to frighten me?"

"Yes, on both counts." His voice was dead serious.

Taylor knew what she was seeing, but was having a hard time believing it. A gun pointed at her was out of context in her life experience. It didn't make sense.

"This way," Donald said with a wave of his gun. "To my office."

Taylor froze. All she could do was look at the gun.

"Please don't make me ask you again."

"Fine, I'll have a drink with you," she said flippantly and marched to his office. For one moment she played with the idea of running up the stairs, but if he really meant to shoot her she wouldn't have a chance. Better to play this out until Jim came back. She hoped he wouldn't be long.

"Sit."

Taylor did so, on the chair nearest the door. Donald returned the gun to his pocket. She watched in fascination as Donald placed his kettle on a hot plate and warmed the water.

"Please keep in mind Taylor, you can't get away." He patted the pocket.

Donald took two cups from his desk. How ironic that

both cups had a happy face on the side. In each he dropped a tea bag. They were not the kind you buy in a grocery store, but the type you buy and fill yourself.

It bothered her that it had taken this long to realize Donald was the killer. And he was preparing to kill her too. It was so matter of fact, the way it came to her mind. Once she had been in a car accident. When she understood the car was about to slide into hers there was only one thought; it's going to hit. Funny how complicated life is until you're in danger; then it's all so simple.

She thought what to do. Jim would be back at any moment. All she had to do was stall.

"How did you get the paint on Jim's overalls?"

He raised his eyebrows and studied her. She would not look away from his eyes. His usually soft, meekly veiled eyes had a dark and steely gaze now.

"I used them to climb in the window," he said.

"What window?"

"Endicott's window," Donald said. "I had to leave it open because his office door needed to remain locked; and to retrieve the envelopes."

"But why? The poison was on Jessica's return envelope."

"I applied the poison to all the envelopes, just to make certain he licked at least one of them. But in order to implicate Jessica I wanted the other envelopes out of his office. When I climbed up the painter's ladder to get them, there was fresh paint on the wall."

"You also killed Dominique?"

The water was boiling and Taylor watched him fill the cups. Steam rose from each as the basement was cool.

"That witch and her locked-room murder mystery," Donald said. "I had to slow down the publication of her latest rag."

He stirred each cup in turn.

"But she didn't know anything. I read her manuscript. It wasn't about Preston's mur . . . murder." Taylor didn't know how much longer she could go on talking. It was all she could do to control her terror and have a polite conversation with a madman.

"I couldn't take a chance you see. She had to go."

"Why kill Preston in the first place? I don't understand any of this."

"Don't you? You visited my mother. Yes, I knew you were there snooping. You saw the family photos. I don't look like the rest of my family. My looks came from my father; old man Endicott."

"Preston Endicott was your father? But that means . . ."

"That junior was my half-brother. You see, I knew you'd figure it out."

"But why him?"

"Because the money dear old dad left us when he died was gone; eaten up with Mother's maladies. I can't even live on my own. The money always goes to medicine and hospital stays. With him gone, I could step in and claim the estate."

"But Preston hadn't taken Jessica out of his will, and she inherited most of the personal estate and the business," Taylor said.

"She ruined everything. I tried to get her too." He folded his hands on the desk. "Paid her a little visit. Poor thing was sick. I watched her leave the kitchen. She left the door unlocked. I turned on the burners. Thought that would take care of her.

"You just had to go running over there breaking out windows. Yes, I was watching. If you'd minded your own

184

business, she'd have died in a house fire and I wouldn't have another loose end."

"Donald, no. The killing has to stop."

"You're nosy, do you know that? Messing in other people's business, like you're Miss Marple. You've read way too many of those mysteries. The heroine usually finds the bad guy and survives to tell about it, right?"

"Right," Taylor said dreading what he might say next.

Where was Jim? How long had it been? It seemed like hours, but she thought probably only thirty minutes. But that was more than enough time get his car.

"I tried to scare you, but you don't learn."

"You shot out my window?" Taylor felt he was winding down and she didn't want to face the end of his agenda.

"Enough talk," Donald said. "I think I've answered all your questions. Now, drink this. Yours has a special ingredient. You'll notice a slight bitter taste, but I've added sugar. It should be palatable."

"How are you going to explain my death?" Taylor nearly choked on the words.

"Another horrible tragedy in the case. Everyone knew the detective warned you to be careful. As usual, you weren't. Here you are again; alone. Where's your bodyguard?"

"If you're talking about Jim, he is on his way right now." She fervently hoped that was the truth.

"My dear Taylor, surely you don't expect me to believe that?"

Yes, she really hoped he would. She didn't think she could carry on this horrible dialogue much longer. Jim, she willed her mind to reach him. Please get here in time.

Chapter 24

J im wanted to get his car before the storm broke. The deep blue clouds obscured the peaks and spread toward the city. He watched the cotton candy cloud towers turn dark grey. The churning mass was almost black and downpours could be seen against the Jemez range.

Traffic was heavy on Cerrillos which wasn't news. The cab was making little progress. Cerrillos Road was the first exit off of Interstate 25 from Albuquerque and had become Santa Fe's motel row. It was a driver's nightmare, full of signs, motels, businesses, intersections, driveways and enough traffic to challenge even a big city driver.

Jim thought the light at Cordova Road would never change in his favor. It was an intersection to be especially careful in because the New Mexico School for the Deaf was nearby.

Once past the Fairview Cemetery, evening commuters mixed with arriving tourists in a car jam of colossal proportions. Sporadic horns blasted when tempers flared as the bumper-to-bumper creep continued. By the time the cab inched its way past the Indian School, the congestion on St. Michael's Drive had eased.

"Ever been to Greer Garson Theatre?" The cabby asked from the rear view mirror, mistaking Jim for a visitor. He was relaxing with his right arm stretched out across the seat back.

"Many times," Jim said.

"That Greer Garson," the taxi driver continued completely ignoring Jim's reply. "She was some dame. Saw all her movies. *Mrs. Miniver*, 1942, was some flick. She got the Oscar for that one."

Jim groaned. Terrific: a trivia expert. He wasn't around in 1942, hadn't seen the movie and didn't want to. But mostly, he didn't want to talk with this man. He wanted to get his Jeep, yesterday already, but certainly before the rain made it even more difficult to drive. As if to remind him, thunder assaulted his eardrums once again.

"That was close!" the cabby said.

"Can you go any faster?" Jim asked.

"Not and stay within the law."

Since when did speed limits bother cab drivers? Jim tried to sit back and relax, but something besides the delay was bothering him. He wished Taylor had come along with him. He should have known better than to think he could run this errand within thirty minutes at this time of day.

"This the right place?" the driver asked.

"This is it!" Jim shoved some money at him and bounded from the cab.

"Car's 'bout ready," a mechanic in a blue jumpsuit told Jim, wiping his hands on a rag.

"I'm in a hurry. Will it be long?"

"Nah. Few minutes."

Why had they called and said it was ready if it wasn't?

Why hadn't he insisted Taylor come along? He didn't like Sanchez. Okay, he was a bit jealous of him because of Taylor's apparent infatuation. But he had Taylor's best interest at heart when he asked her to stay with someone at all times.

The clouds had moved in overhead and he was certain he could not get back before it opened up. Thunder rumbled close by and one jagged lighting strike cracked open the clouds.

Jim dialed Taylor's phone to let her know he was delayed. It went to voice mail. He left a message, followed it with a text. Why wasn't she answering?

"Kid's bringing it around now," the mechanic yelled. "You gonna pay for this today?"

Jim stood at the counter while the statement was completed by the mechanic, totaled by the bookkeeper, entered into a computer, printed and finally placed in front of him. He scrawled his name on the credit card receipt and hurried to the 4-wheel.

"Oh no!" He slapped the seat in frustration. "I'll never get left in this traffic."

He couldn't explain his feeling of apprehension. Not one to put much stock in things like intuition, he didn't like the anxiety that kept nudging him.

With tires screeching, he turned right and made a dangerous lane change, bumped over the median, followed by an illegal U-turn. He heard a couple of angry horns from drivers he narrowly missed. In a minute, they'd be mad at someone else.

The storm broke with hail and driving rain as he pulled back into the sea of cars on Cerrillos. The quarter-size hail was soft as a snow cone and splattered on his windshield. But hail was the least of his problems. The rain was a torrent and he could barely see even with the wipers working feverishly. He slowed the Jeep to a crawl and inched behind the car in front of him. Before he could get through the intersection the light turned red.

"What else?" Jim, not known for his patience under normal circumstances, was beginning to lose control of his thoughts. It must be the storm, he'd never liked them. When the light went green the cars leading the pack drove like it was a sunny, dry day across flooded streets, splashing water over the curb. When traffic again stopped, he was the second car in line.

"Not again."

Jim was tempted to buck over another curb just to keep moving, but resisted the impulse.

He pulled out his cell phone, placed it on the passenger seat and called Taylor on speaker. It was against the law in Santa Fe to use a cell phone while driving and he didn't want to add a police stop to his list of frustrations.

The only answer was her voice mail.

"Taylor. It's Jim. Call me. Hung up in traffic."

The cars thinned out as he reached downtown. Most folks were going the other way. He bypassed the office parking lot and opted for the sidewalk in front of the building. No one was likely to ticket him. They'd have to get wet to do it. Jim held his jacket over his head as he ran up the steps. There he shivered under the portal while he searched for his key card. When he reached for the door, it opened at his touch. The pit in his stomach seemed to swallow him whole. He'd checked the door twice before he left. It had been locked.

Inside, the office was dark with the exception of the

light that always burned on Candi's desk. A soft glow penetrated the gloom of the basement stairwell. Why was a light on down there? He'd turned them off earlier.

Stepping softly, Jim descended, straining to hear any sounds. He recognized Taylor's voice first.

"Jim will be here any moment."

Something about her voice made him hesitate to call out to her.

* * *

"Is that lily of the valley in the tea?" Taylor stood and pointed at the cup he pushed toward her.

"It is. Have some," Donald said with a slight smile.

"Where did you get it? I didn't see any growing at your house."

"I harvested some I found in the neighborhood, dried and hid it. I'm good at hiding things. No one suspects a dull, boring accountant of anything."

She considered distracting him so she could switch the cups. They both looked alike with their smiling faces. She took a step forward as if to take the proffered cup, tripped over her own feet and dropped the note pads. Several went tumbling toward Donald. Instinctively he reached to retrieve them, caught himself and stopped.

"Nice try," he said. Donald watched her intently. She'd blown her only opportunity.

Jim watched from the dark shadows of the stairwell. The hall light was on and Donald's desk lamp was lit. He assumed Donald was in his office with Taylor, but he could see only her back. She dropped something and picked it up. Something was off. He waited.

Taylor wished she dared to scream. She was convinced he would shoot the moment she opened her mouth. No one would hear her anyway. They would have to be right outside the window to pick up a scream in this storm. Even if someone was outside they'd be in a big hurry to get out of the rain. No, it would have to be real loud, like Jessica's deafening alarm.

Instead she said, "For a guy clever enough to plan a locked-room murder, this tea party is quite clumsy."

"My methods are none of your concern," Donald said with steel in his voice. "Drink it or I will shoot you and be done with this."

If only the security system was set she could move back a few steps and cross the eye of the motion detector. The alarm would make a racket that would bring the police. She'd thought it silly when Jessica installed a separate system in the basement, but she would have given a lot at that moment to have it blasting. But it wasn't set, and the keypad was at the base of the steps. She glanced in the direction of the stairwell and noticed someone standing there in the shadows.

It was Jim!

She felt relief spread over her, but he continued to stand there. Why didn't he save her or at least call the police? He wasn't yet aware of the jeopardy she was facing.

Taylor stretched her arms behind her and pointed one index finger in the direction of the motion detector placed high on the wall.

Jim watched as Taylor backed up a couple of steps and seemed to point at something near the ceiling. The passageway through the basement was lined with his and Donald's office on one side and several metal storage cabinets, a table and old stacked files. A couple of non-descript pictures hung from the wall.

"Taylor," Donald said. "I'm waiting. There is no way out. Drink it." He pushed the cup across the table.

In a last desperate move she did the hand trick again, and then punched her finger against her back with the hope it looked like someone coding a keypad. She glanced at Jim.

"Donald, I don't want to drink the poison." She said it loud and clear. Jim had to hear her.

"Oh lordy," Jim muttered. His gut instinct had been right. Taylor was in trouble. But what was the pointing about? He looked at the wall on his left again, but this time scanned all the way to the ceiling. The only thing above the cabinets was the motion detector.

The motion detector!

Now he understood the finger dance on her back. He punched buttons furiously on the pad.

"Oh no. That's not it." He canceled and started over.

Taylor was about to try the hand signals again, but it was too late. Donald was pushing the cup into her hand. If she let him get any closer he would see Jim and then it would be over for both of them. She took the cup and glanced at Jim. Much to her relief he was madly programming the pad. It would beep shortly.

"I still don't understand why you think you have to kill me? Don't you know the police will catch you? You'll spend the rest of your life in the penitentiary."

She continued to babble. "And what will happen to your mother? You know she's a very special person, don't you? She raised you all by herself; you have an education, a good job . . ."

"What was that?" Donald started.

It was the alarm beep as it set. Jim had come through.

"I didn't hear anything. It must be the storm."

She began to back up, very slowly, towards the motion detector's vision.

"That's enough. Drink it."

Jim reached for his phone. His pocket was empty. He'd left the cell in his Jeep. He raced up the steps and lunged for Candi's phone knocking over her lamp. Her telephone had buttons all over it. After a moment of indecision he pushed the first line and dialed the police. He described what was happening, gave the address and asked for Sanchez. The receiver missed the cradle as he hurried back downstairs to help Taylor.

Taylor raised the cup slowly. She continued to take small steps backward; it didn't seem to bother him. He was only intent that she drink the tea. She must have passed the beam by now; in a few seconds it would . . . she threw the cup at Donald and ran for Jim's office as the siren wailed. It must have scared the bejesus out of Donald. He jumped straight up and struggled to get the gun.

Taylor dove into Jim's office next door, slammed the door and locked it. It would take several minutes before the police arrived and she didn't think the door would hold if he started firing at it. Adrenalin rushed through her body. She piled furniture against the door. Jim's roll-around file cabinet was first. It jammed under the doorknob. One arm cleared the desk in a neat sweep. Pencils, papers, markers and a half-filled coffee cup scattered. She shoved one end of the desk until it bumped against the pile of furniture. As Donald fired two shots through the door, Taylor ducked under the desk and covered her head.

Jim was almost down the stairs when he heard the shots. He flattened himself against the wall in the darkness and crept down the last few steps. Donald stood firing shots through his office door. Jim looked for something to throw at him, but he would have to enter the basement and risk being shot. He hoped Taylor was okay.

The next minutes were the most frightening of her life. Taylor couldn't be sure how many bullets his gun held. Most of the mysteries she read had guns with six chambers. Jim couldn't possibly try to rescue her now, not with Donald shooting up the place. A bullet zinged within a foot of her right shoulder and lodged in the thin inner wall behind her. After everything she'd been through it looked like Donald might still win.

Then it all hit the fan. She couldn't be sure with all the noise and the storm, but it sounded like police sirens outside. Finally!

She heard things like "Drop it! Police. Hands up."

There were sounds of scuffle. Donald's angry protestations, "I'm his son. I deserved it."

Then there was Jim's sweet voice, full of concern, even fear.

"Taylor, you all right?" He slammed his body against the door.

"I'm okay," she shouted. "The door is blocked. I'll have to move your desk."

She pushed and shoved, but she no longer had all the adrenalin. It took a few minutes to clear the door. Taylor opened it, saw Jim and rushed into his arms.

When they reached the lobby, Donald was gone and several officers stood at the front doors.

She perched on the arm of the reception sofa. Her legs threatened to fold.

Victor Sanchez flew through the door. An officer nodded in her direction. He made no attempt to conceal his concern.

"Taylor, are you all right?"

Taylor tried for a smile. It didn't feel quite right.

"I'm fine."

"She's not fine," Jim interjected. "She was nearly killed."

"Why didn't you call me?" Victor admonished her and ignored Jim. "That's what I'm here for. How can I convince you to pick up the phone?"

"It would have been rude to make a phone call during a tea party. Besides, my cell is in my office."

"Do you know what she's talking about?" To Jim.

"Sure. It was a dark and stormy night which nearly ended in a fatal tea party," Jim said angry. "Donald is the murderer."

"I'll need statements from you both at the station."

"Tonight?" Jim said. "Come on Sanchez. A lunatic just tried to kill her. Can the detective stuff."

"Okay, tomorrow."

"Taylor, I'll take you home," Jim said.

"No, I want to go by myself. I'll take a cab. I need to be alone.

"Thank you Jim. Thank you." Taylor wrapped her arms around him.

"Don't thank me," he said pushing her gently back. "It was your idea. I only wish it hadn't taken me so long to figure out what you were trying to tell me." He kissed her cheek and left.

She rose to go but before she could pass him Victor caught her in the strongest arms since her father's. His uniform was soaked with rain and he smelled faintly of piñon smoke.

"I'll tell you all about it in the morning. Right now, I'd like to go home. I've got a cat to feed."

195

Chapter 25

The following weekend, Taylor and Victor sat in front of a warm crackling fire at the Pink Adobe. It was a popular restaurant and a bit expensive for his tastes; but he wanted to take Taylor someplace special. They'd started in the Dragon Room, the restaurant's bar. It was a unique place, nationally known. Trees held up the roof. They had long ago died, but the trunks made for interesting repartee. It was small but usually had entertainment. After drinks they'd settled in comfortably in the dining room. He'd hoped for a patio table, but it was a cold autumn evening and they found the fire most welcoming.

"Sure is nice to relax. Even Oscar doesn't seem as tense. He senses the crisis is over."

"Just wish we had all the loose ends neatly tied," Victor said.

"For instance, I don't know who Dominique was with that night at La Fonda. Or, if it's even important."

"With her death we may never know," Taylor said.

"Right. The odd thing about Donald Lovitt," Victor

said. "He was not the son of the elder Endicott."

"What! But he said he was. That was why he killed Preston, Jr. and Dominique."

"We questioned Mrs. Lovitt, with her doctor present. She said Endicott had been a friend of hers, they might have been lovers at one time, but she didn't say as much. But he was definitely not Donald's father. She had his birth certificate to prove it. That was something Donald fabricated over years of loneliness and deprivation, with some considerable circumstantial evidence to back up his delusions. He grew to resent his mother, whose medical care took most of his income."

"What will happen to him?" Taylor asked.

"Oh, he'll serve time, and lot's of it."

"I still can't believe he killed two people and tried to kill me, for nothing."

"Unfortunately, it happens more often than any of us would want to believe. The mind does horrible things to the despairing and lonely."

"What about the tan car?" Taylor asked. "You know, the one I saw all over town."

"It was rented by Donald. I suppose to throw suspicion on Virginia. He hasn't said as much, but we located the rental agreement at the Albuquerque airport. The car was listed as missing."

"And Dominique? She didn't know a thing about Donald. All she did was write a mystery."

"There's something else about Dominique," Victor said. "Remember we found the manuscripts by Dannie Beldon?"

"Sure, in her studio."

"At first we though Dannie Beldon was Dominique's real name. She changed hers legally to Dominique Boucher from Donna Beldon."

197

"I can understand why; nowhere near flashy enough for our Dominique."

"I'm still checking, but I suspect there may be a sister or other family member by that name," Victor said.

"The woman at Dominique's memorial service? The one no one knew? I couldn't see her with the veil so I can't tell you what she looked like. We thought she was a fan who managed to get past the gates."

"The case is officially closed. It's up to the courts now."

"So Dominique was not her real name. She chose Boucher after Anthony Boucher."

"Who's he?" Victor asked.

"Anthony Boucher was a mystery writer. The world mystery convention, Bouchercon, was named in his honor."

"I see I have a lot to learn about mysteries."

"Maybe I can pick up a few things from you on criminal investigations."

"Taylor," Victor said with suspicion. "I don't like the sound of that. What are you thinking?"

"Just to use in my job; the more I know about police work the better judge I'll be of mysteries." At that moment, feeling safe and happy with Victor smiling across the table, Taylor believed she meant it.

Victor lifted his wine glass.

"To mysteries."

"To mysteries."

Epilogue

Donald Lovitt was convicted of murder on two counts, and the attempted murders of Jessica and Taylor. He was sentenced to life in the New Mexico state penitentiary. Jessica Endicott established a trust for Mrs. Lovitt. She now lives in an assisted living community. On good days she works in their greenhouse. Virginia Compton is back as senior editor, doing the work she loves. She and Jessica seem to have come to an understanding. There are rumors Jim Wells may be moving back upstairs. Piñon Publishing's future looks bright, but they are in the market for a new mystery writer. Victor Sanchez was almost sorry to see the case closed. He finds his thoughts turning to Taylor Browning with increasing frequency. She once again enjoys sunsets on the deck with Oscar who is now being fed on time. Feline incidents are on the decline. Taylor's not so sure the restful life is what she wants anymore.

Did you enjoy *Dead Editor File?*

If so, please consider writing a short review on Amazon or Goodreads. Thank you for reading *Dead Editor File*, the first in the Taylor Browning Cozy Mystery Series.
G G Collins

ABOUT THE
AUTHOR

G G Collins worked for a book publisher before she walked a reporter's beat. Take this experience; add a mystery, a feline companion and you get a new cozy mystery series.

Collins has been cat mom to a dozen kitties, all with their own eccentricities. Oscar is the reincarnation of her late Abyssinian cat. Somehow her pets in spirit live on in her storytelling. She also loves and writes about horses.

Dead Editor File is the first in the Taylor Browning Cozy Mysteries, followed by *Looking Glass Editor*. Collins currently has three books in the Rachel Blackstone Paranormal Mysteries (*Reluctant Medium, Lemurian Medium & Atomic Medium*). She has written two young adult novels: An equestrian teen lit book entitled *Flying Change* and *Without Notice,* a story of loss and renewal. All are available on Amazon.

Book Blog:
https://reluctantmediumatlarge.wordpress.com/

News, Views & Reviews Blog:
https://paralleluniverseatlarge.wordpress.com/

Follow on Twitter: @GGCollinsWriter
https://twitter.com/GGCollinsWriter

46917746R00128

Made in the USA
Middletown, DE
03 June 2019